Cross Your Heart,
Connie Pickles

∞

SABINE DURRANT

Cross Your Heart, Connie Pickles

HarperTempest
An Imprint of HarperCollinsPublishers

HarperTempest is an imprint of HarperCollins Publishers.

Cross Your Heart, Connie Pickles
Copyright © 2005 by Sabine Durrant
All rights reserved. Printed in the United States of America.
No part of this book may be used or reproduced in any manner whatsoever
without written permission except in the case of brief quotations embodied
in critical articles and reviews. For information address HarperCollins
Children's Books, a division of HarperCollins Publishers,
1350 Avenue of the Americas, New York, NY 10019.
www.harperteen.com

Library of Congress Cataloging-in-Publication Data is available.
ISBN-10: 0-06-085479-0 (trade bdg.)
ISBN-13: 978-0-06-085479-9 (trade bdg.)
ISBN-10: 0-06-085480-4 (lib. bdg.)
ISBN-13: 978-0-06-085480-5 (lib. bdg.)

Typography by Larissa Lawrynenko
1 2 3 4 5 6 7 8 9 10
❖
Originally published in 2005 by Penguin Books Ltd, London, England
First U.S. Edition, HarperCollins Publishers, 2007

For my friend Hilary

Welcome to the very private notebook of Constance de Bellechasse. Also known as Connie Pickles. Please, please don't read this without the permission of its owner. Especially if you are its owner's mother, little brother or sister, or if you are William. Or Jack. Or Mr. Spence. Constance de Bellechasse accepts *no* responsibility for any embarrassment, blushing, or crossness resulting from reading this notebook!

Signed: *Connie Pickles*

Chapter One

SUNDAY, FEBRUARY 9
The roof, midnight

I've just written my name on the outside of this book and I wish I hadn't. It's midnight and I was feeling all romantic and blustery, and now I feel cross. Connie Pickles is *not* how I see myself. Constance de Bellechasse is how I see myself. It's a good thing I'm writing this in the open air, and very high up, or I'd feel quite cast down.

I'm on the roof, you see. It's freezing and I should be in bed, but I couldn't sleep and I hate wasting time. I'm wearing my striped men's pajamas, two sweaters, my bathrobe, and a pair of socks, so I'm quite warm. There are clouds wisping across the dark sky, tangerine from the streetlights. The moon is right above my head—it's a sort of semicircle, but it's tipped on its side, and if it wasn't for the wind and the weird orange clouds blowing against it, you might think it would lose its balance altogether.

I'm not going to lose my balance. Or throw myself off. Don't worry. I'm always on the roof, so I'm used to it. It's my favorite place in the whole world. You can see all the gardens of the houses in our street laid out in little rows, and the gardens of the street that backs on to ours. You can even see my friend William's window if you *crane*. I'm always telling him he should climb out too, but his roof hasn't got a flat part and he says he's not breaking his neck just to wave to me, thank you very much. It's not dangerous at my end, but you have to be careful. The only tricky thing is getting here. You have to climb on the bed and then bend and jump up at the same time. You can't overshoot, but sometimes I scrape my back on the window frame. In summer, too, it can get really hot because it's asphalt. Tonight it's cool and soft like the skin of an apple.

Oh, there you go. I'm doing it again. I'm trying to be all poetic. And I've vowed not to; this delicious new diary is to have none of that. The thing is, I'm not poetic. Or romantic. Or, much as I'd like to be, French. De Bellechasse is only my mother's maiden name. And Connie is what everybody calls me. Not Constance. Just plain, dowdy, clumsy Connie. As for France, I've only ever been there once, on the school trip to Boulogne. And that was only for a day.

I'm Connie Pickles and that's that.

Or is it?

Because something *big* hit me this evening. I've been reading this book called *The Blessing* by Nancy Mitford, and there's this small boy in it who decides to take his mother's life in hand. Well, it set me thinking, and when I went down for supper—cheese on toast (again)—and Marie and Cyril wouldn't go to bed, charging around like bulls in a . . . well, in a small rented house, and there was Mother in her threadbare black suit, flicking through a six-month-old French *Vogue* someone left on the Tube, looking vague and fragile and tired, it made me think. Just because I'm only fourteen, it doesn't mean I can't make things happen.

My dream used to be to reunite her with her parents, my grandparents, *les* de Bellechasses. They're French and very grand. But they cut her off when she met my father, who was a penniless actor/pizza delivery man. He died and now she won't speak to them. She never opens their letters. And she gets so cross when I ask her about them . . . So no, I think it will have to be something else. I think it will have to be a New Man.

It would be okay if I could trust her to find someone for herself, but she can't. She works in a lingerie shop to make ends meet—which they don't *quite*—and a bra shop, no matter how royally appointed, is not the best venue for meeting men. Also she has terrible taste. My father was very handsome. And Mother assures me he was a brilliant actor. But I can't help wondering—if he was such a brilliant actor, what was he doing delivering pizzas on the night he died? As for her second husband, Jack, sweetie that he is—and I know Marie and Cyril adore him—he's just not reliable.

The moon has gone behind a cloud. And I just yawned, which is a giveaway. I'm going to climb into bed now. The thing is not to worry about how things are, but to bring about change. That's why I've started this notebook, this beautiful notebook with its crisp pages and delicious smell—I bought it on that trip to Boulogne (I love stationery)—although there are still some pages left in the old one. This notebook is a book with a purpose. With serious intent. It is a campaign diary. I hereby declare my resolution to put our lives in order, to find Mother a man. Requirements: 1) Money. 2) Experience with small children. 3) French connections.

Constance de Bellechasse . . . oh, all right, Connie Pickles is on the case.

Chapter Two

MONDAY, FEBRUARY 10
8:30 a.m.

*U*sual chaos at breakfast. Quick scribble to repeat intentions before school.

Cyril and Marie are fighting over the *Beano* Jack brought around the other day. Breakfast is from the Tupperware where Mother collects the stuff no one will eat from the bottom of the cereal box: muesli dust and cornflake pap. It saves a lot on wastage, but it does tend to lower the spirits. Cyril has spilled milk on his trousers. We've run out of cat food and Dave, our tabby, is winding around everyone's legs hopefully. The sofa bed, where Mother sleeps, is still out in the sitting room. The radio's on. There is talk of a war and a "long shadow over the economy." (That's just what I need.) And Mr. Spence, our landlord, has dropped in.

I opened the door and physically barred his entry.

"Hello?" I said suspiciously. Marie scrawled felt-tip marker on the radiator the other day; I thought it might be best if he didn't see that. Also he was wearing a T-shirt made out of blue string and the smallest pair of satin shorts you've ever seen, so I didn't really want him in the house. His face glowed sweatily and there was a little drip on the end of his nose. He was jogging up and down on the spot as if he didn't intend to hang around.

But then Mother bustled up behind me and said, "Mr. Spence, enter, enter, enter." (She often says things in threes.) She put her lipstick on the moment she heard the door. She is all woman where all men are concerned.

He stopped jogging and said, "John, please. As I'm always saying," and she almost *simpered*. She was wearing her cheap brown suit, with a little pink T-shirt underneath. (She is always, always elegant, unlike me. She has a knack with color.) Marie had been fiddling with her hair—putting in those sparkle things you twist in—and Mother had just been tickling Cyril to cheer him on with his breakfast, so there was a flush to her cheeks and she really looked lovely. And there was Mr. Spence with his pale, hairless thighs and his hopeful, droopy expression and his damp satin shorts (frankly, I had to avert my eyes).

William will be calling for me any minute—we bike to school together—and I'm not happy. Mr. Spence is inspecting the leaking kitchen roof and Mother's out in the garden hovering prettily by his bare legs. I don't know what she's playing at. It's time she took the children to school. They're going to be late. Marie gets in a tizzy if she misses attendance, and Cyril's got his SATs this year and everything. But she's still out there flirting with him.

Honestly, if anything is going to galvanize me into action, this is.

ß

SAME DAY
Geography, period five

Push and Pull Factors. We've got a substitute teacher, so no one's paying any attention. Karen and Josie—aka The Shazzers—are in the corner fiddling with their gold jewelry. The Grungers are all buried in their headphones. And Joseph Milton, who's said to be the scariest boy in our class (though not by me: he was at Our Lady of Victories, so I've known him since he had to keep a spare pair of pants in his cubby), is kissing his teeth at the teacher suggestively. And Julie, my best friend, has got her head down as if she is working hard. Only I know she isn't.

I found her at break and we sat on the bench near the concrete pit where some of the boys do their skateboarding.

Her in her cool parka with the fake-fur collar, me in my pink pack-a-mac (bargain at Cancer Research). Recently the skateboarding seems to have been a bit more show-offy when Julie is on the bench. It's not that she's pretty exactly. She's got large features—a huge nose and a jutting chin and big lips that she licks a lot. But she's womanly, if you know what I mean. She wears a proper bra, not just an undershirt like me. And she doesn't care what people think. She says I don't either or I wouldn't wear wellies and pink pack-a-macs to school. But I wear wellies and pink pack-a-macs to school because I *do* care what people think. There's not enough money for me to buy trendy stuff, so I'd rather opt out altogether. I'd rather be wacky than boring. Thrift-shop chic, I call it. Anyway, back to Julie. Not caring is why I think she's so popular. William says it has more to do with certain other Large Features. That boy can be so childish.

I knew I could tell her about my plan to find Mother a boyfriend and that she would take it in hand. She's really good at things like that. She's more clued up than me romantically. She's had two boyfriends herself, one of them, Phil from the sixth-form college, quite serious. I saw them in the high street at Christmas outside HMV. He had his hand up her sweater. I had to run home and eat chocolate to get over the shock.

"Hm," she said when I explained and ran through my

requirements (quick recap—money, interest in France, ability to handle small children). "Int-er-est-ing." She rolled the word out in a sort of French manner, and took a drag of her cigarette. I don't smoke, by the way. Julie does. It is one of the many differences between us. We met on the very first day of junior high after she stood up for me when some girls in the eighth grade started throwing my tartan beret around and calling me names. "Freak yourself!" she said over her shoulder as she took my arm. We've been friends ever since.

At break she gave me a long look. Her eyes under the black eyeliner were very pale green, like the Wedgwood ashtray Mother and Jack got for a wedding present. She's a bit funny about parents and their other halves. She puts on a voice when she talks about her stepmother. Like, "Ali-son thinks Dad should take us out to TGI Friday's tomorrow night," and although I know she loves TGI Friday's, there's something in the way she leaves the sentence hanging as if even she doesn't know what she wants from it that makes you wonder. So I didn't know whether she might be about to tell me not to be stupid or something. But then she grinned. "I think we can have fun with this," she said. "Leave it with me. Double geog. Substitute teacher. I need something to keep me busy."

She's just passed me a note. "Walk me to the bus stop after school. I've made a list."

Blissful hour to myself before Jack's mother, Granny Enid, who looks after Marie and Cyril straight from school, drops them back. It's v peaceful if I close my eyes to the loose felt-tip marker and abandoned socks, to the damp spot on the kitchen ceiling. Bit hungry, though. There's not much in the cupboard, but I found a package of rice cakes. Some people think rice cakes are just cardboard, but if you concentrate on them, you can persuade yourself they're quite delicious. It's important not to compare them to other things, like chocolate cookies, that's all.

I have stuff to record. Operation New Man is under way.

Julie and I met at the sheds and we walked down the hill together—or rather, she walked; I rolled alongside her with my hand on and off the brakes. It wasn't until the bus stop that she got out her list. This is what it said:

1. *"MONSIEUR" BAKER*
   Don't! Wait a moment before you move on. I
   know a teacher is a weird suggestion, but look
   beyond the hair (lack of) and the peculiar walk.
   Put the "Non, non, non, Mademoiselle" out of

your head. Think: culture. Think: connections.
Think: already-speaks-the-lingo. He's the right
age—forty, d'ya reck?—he's single, and he's got a
mobile home in the Dordogne. Don't puke; I'm
thinking of you here, babe.

2. MY UNCLE BERT

Soo rich, sooo cool, soooo going out with
someone else. She's ghastly. We can fix it. Just
imagine yourself living it up in his Chelsea
penthouse. He says he can get me two comps for
the Electric B'stards at the Palais on Friday. Any
point me asking if you want to come? His only
fault: an overdependency on cKone aftershave.

3. NEW PHARMACIST GUY

The hunky one in the old Levi's who's always up
a ladder. Either he owns the shop (i.e., financial
security, long-term prospects), or he's just passing
through (traveler/artist/possibly recovering drug
addict, in which case toss him). Good bum,
though (got to count for something).

4. ANY EXES?

Over to you here, Con. Is there anyone that may
have slipped the net? We mustn't overlook the

obvious, e.g., wasn't there some lush bloke she
met on the Tube last year?

Julie was watching me as I read the list, with her head cocked on one side like an expectant dog. I looked at her. Then I said, "Monsieur Baker. No way."

Julie said she knew I was going to say that.

"No way," I said again. "No way."

I put my head back and slunk, as if slowly dying, to the ground. I made a few choking noises while I was down there. I had a momentary vision of meeting him in the bathroom doorway, him with a towel on. . . .

Julie turned to Margaret Jackson, who was next in the bus line. "Mushroom bake," she said. "Always stick to cold food in the cafeteria."

Then she kicked me, and I stood up.

"I'm not joking," she said. "I've thought it through. *You* don't have to fancy him. Only your mom does. And just think: Monsieur Baker's life ambition is to retire to France. Nuff said. Think about it."

I nodded and said I would, but then her bus came and she got on and, as it shunted up to the lights alongside me, I did the Baker walk—a heavy marionette sort of galumph, sausages for limbs—resting my tongue on my lower lip at the same time (which was a bit unfair because, while he does funnel up his mouth when he speaks French, he doesn't actually do that). Julie sat looking out of the bus window, shaking her head at me in pity.

She's right, though, he's worth considering. Okay, I've considered him. No.

We didn't get a chance to talk about the rest of her list. She said to ring her tonight. Here's what I think:

HER UNCLE: hm. Careful: Julie adores him. Boyish body, haggard face, yoof-ful clothes. Would he fill our house with the spirit of maturity I'm after? Would he make Mother happy? Perhaps. I've only met him once or twice, the last time at Julie's mom's Christmas cocktail party. He had his girlfriend with him—one of those karmically poised women with hair that's a bit too long for their face. He kept putting his hands inside her waistband at the back, which was a bit yuk. A possible.

PHARMACIST GUY: you only ever get to see bits of him—bejeaned bum up a ladder (good spot, Jules), or a corner of his face through the little window at the back. I'll have to get a full-frontal. Save a fortune on dental floss.

AS FOR EXES . . . Mother's a disaster on the romance front. The men she meets are either homeless or hapless or, like the man on the Tube, married. And not Jack, please. I know that would make a wonderfully happy ending, but it's not going to happen here. They are so ill-suited. Mother needs someone to provide order in her life, while Jack . . . Jack's not just serially unfaithful. He's always got some new mad plan—the latest one's selling fish door to door (he pretends it comes from Newcastle)—but he's never got quite enough "at this precise moment in time" to pay the bills.

Oh, I really ought to be able to think of a wonderful future husband for her myself. (There should be a big gap here to indicate the ten minutes I have just spent staring at the ceiling.) But I can't.

Doorbell. I'm not allowed to open the front door if I'm alone in the house. Something has just rattled through the letter box. I'll just go and see what.

ℰ

My bedroom, 10 p.m.

Might have guessed: chocolate. William and I have a thing about chocolate. It's like a private joke without the joke.

I opened the door and he was standing on the mat, looking sheepish and irritating. He'd just got off his bike—the skin on his face and arms was mottled red and white as if he was hot and cold at the same time. The chain with his crucifix was out of his T-shirt, skew-whiff across his shoulder.

He said, "Where were you? I waited for you at the sheds."

Bother. We usually cycle home together and I'd forgotten to tell him I was walking with Julie. I should have felt guilty, but I just felt cross. I said, "I went with Julie."

"Oh," he said, looking hurt. "Oh, sorry."

He's always apologizing, even when I'm at fault. It's a vicious circle we're in. I'm hoity-toity; he's repentant. And the awful thing is, the nicer he is, the crosser I get. I'm really not a very nice person.

"Do you want to come in, then?" I said.

"Yeah, all right."

He wheeled his bike into the hall, leaned it against mine, and followed me into the kitchen. His jeans are so wide and baggy these days the legs seem to start down at his knees. He's such a fashion victim. Sometimes I think I'm outgrowing him.

He sat on the stool while I filled the kettle. "Did you hear about the French exchange?" he said.

I stopped what I was doing. "No. I didn't have French today."

"Yeah," he said casually. "Easter holidays. You have

to get your form in by the end of the week. Check for eighty quid. I doubt I'll bother."

I turned around and he was looking at me closely. He knows how I feel about France—the de Bellechasse thing—that it's my spiritual home. (In fact, it annoys him; he thinks it's pretentious.) I felt sick.

"Eighty quid?" I said.

"Yeah. Probably not worth the hassle."

I sat down next to him. "How does it work?"

"Two weeks at Easter with a family in Paris. Then the French student comes back to you in the summer."

"Two weeks in Paris?" My heart soared. I imagined myself reunited with my grandparents, an elegant woman in a bun clasping me to her bosom, a small dog at her heels. Two weeks in Paris!

William was still looking at me. He said, "Yeah. Probably not worth—"

How could I ask Mother for eighty quid? "No," I agreed, trying not to sound miserable. "No, it's probably not." I stared at the table. I remembered the day trip to Boulogne with the school, how I envied the neat French schoolgirls in their brown suede boots. Even the stationery shop where I bought this notebook was heavenly. "Do you want a rice cake?" I said. "They're not exactly chocolate cookies, but . . ."

William was opening the package of chocolates. "Ah,

but we could be inventive!" he said cheerfully. He was probably trying to get me off the French exchange. "We could try melting these on top."

We had a bit of trouble with charring. And clouds of dark gray smoke started pouring out of the grill at one point. But it wasn't completely unsuccessful. Heated-up chocolates go sort of powdery rather than melty. Chocolate rice cakes are not quite as good as chocolate cookies, but they're not bad. When we had a pile each and had put the burned tea towels in some water in the sink, we took them with our cups of tea upstairs to the roof. There's just enough room for us both, though it's squashier than it used to be—must be all the fabric in William's trousers. It was a bit cold—a high blue sky darkening over the roofs—so we pulled the duvet out and tucked it around our knees. We had our usual vague munching chat—the stultifying dullness of suburbia, why substitute teachers are always Australian. We didn't talk anymore about the French exchange, and I didn't tell him about my campaign for Mother. We never do talk about things like that.

I had stopped feeling irritated with him. He's like a different person out of school. Or maybe he's the same, I just look at him differently. There are signs of hair growth on his chin these days and under his nose. I know he shaves sometimes, but he'd hate it if I knew. He's had his hair cut too short—it's the kind of cut that makes old ladies cross the road when they see him. And this evening he looked pale. When he yawned for about the fifth time, I said he needed an early night. He said he'd had one last night, only . . . He trailed off and I said, "Didn't you sleep well?" and he said no, he hadn't. He gave a humph of a laugh. I said, "Did you get woken up?" and he stopped laughing. "A bit," he said, scratching his neck and looking up at the sky.

When Jack lived with us, before the Great Infidelity, he used to say he'd go around and sort William's mom and dad out—or his dad, anyway. All I remember from the sleepovers is the sound of shouting and glass being smashed and William telling me to put my head under the pillow. In the morning, his mother was really friendly and let us have Extra-Thick Single Cream on our Rice Krispies. Once I saw bits of broken glass in the garbage and an empty whisky bottle by the sink.

Jack doesn't talk about going around to sort them out anymore. Maybe he thinks William's old enough to look after himself, which is awful because he can't even look after his hamster. It got out this morning. He thinks it's gone under the floorboards.

Granny Enid dropped C and M back just after William left, and then Mother got into one of her sporadic efficient moods. It usually means she's feeling cheerful. Sometimes she comes in really tired. If she's had a hard day at the shop—"a long, long, long day," when there's been a run on cup sizes or something—she stretches out in a chair, with her dark head back, her bony white throat showing, her high-heeled shoes dangling. Then she'll smile and get up quickly, slip on her slippers, and jolly everyone up, but for a moment in her eyes it's as if she doesn't notice what's going on around her, as if her head and her heart are elsewhere. And that's when I think what a waste it is that she should be stuck at home with three children (or two children and me— I'm very old for my age) when she is so very frail and beautiful.

But there was none of that today. She got the children to bed and then she gave a rapid little clap of her hands and said, "Okay, young lady, homework, no?"

"No," I said. "I've done it."

She looked a bit disappointed, but soon started chatting about her day. Apparently, she served an "agitated man in a suit' who wanted "a set" for his fiancée. Mother said, "Do you mean a brassiere or a camisole? With panties? French panties, briefs, or thong?" You have to imagine the rolled "r's" in that. They make it even more embarrassing.

Well, he blushed to his roots—his face was "red, red, red"—and started muttering about sizes. Here's a trade secret: men always overestimate the extent of their girl-friends' bosoms and underestimate the extent of their bottoms. (My mother is quite petite but, because she knows her stuff, some of her pants are enormous.) So, Mother applied fitter's law and supplied him with a 34C and a medium thong. And then—he bent his head and kissed her hand! In front of her boss and everything! So, now I understand her cheerful mood. "Ooh la!" she said, leaning back into the sofa and flushing at the memory.

We watched the news—more gloom and war in a far-off place—and I thought about mentioning the French exchange. But then she got out her mending—she's adding some old material to the bottom of Cyril's jeans to make them last another year—and she sighed, the man with the set forgotten, and I knew I couldn't. Instead, I sneaked into the kitchen to ring Julie to tell her what I think of her list—Mr. Baker a no-no, Uncle Bert and The Pharmacist to be pursued further—and she's cooking up a plan. We had to be short and sweet because her mom yelled that the pizzas had come. "Oh, sorry, Con," she said. I told her not to worry. We don't have pizzas delivered at our house out of respect to my father, but it doesn't mean other people can't. We're going to talk tomorrow.

I'm up in my room now, with the cat on the end of my bed. Mother and I watched my dad's video before I came up. It's only thirty seconds long. You see him running along a jetty in the sunset, in shorts, with a couple of other young men. He's the one with the curly dark hair and the cheeky grin in the cut-off jeans. He's only about twenty-five. He's laughing and horsing around with his pretend friends and then they all jump off the jetty into the water. It's nice to see him happy. Even if it is in an ad for a vodka-based alcopop. Mother and I joined in with the slogan at the end. "Make a splash!" we cried. "Drink Carrrrib-vod."

I ran her a bath after that. I added rose and geranium oil, which is really for special occasions, like A Date.

" 'Night," I said.

"Sweet dreams, *chérie*," she answered, up to her neck in suds.

Chapter Three

TUESDAY, FEBRUARY 11
The bathroom, 8:30 p.m.

Julie made me cut period six! I've never cut a class in my whole life. Nerds don't. It's how we get to be nerds (even weird ones). But friendship with me demands a lot of compromise if you're someone like Julie, and I know when it's my turn. She collared me the moment I got to school and pulled me into the girls' bathroom. "I thought we'd start with The Pharmacist," she said. "Today. Fact-finding mission. Meet me behind the science block at three-oh-five p.m. I've brought the gear. You don't have to worry about anything. Just be there."

So I was. I was feeling a bit low because Mr. Baker had handed me my French-exchange letter and I knew I'd have to hide it from Mother. But I cheered up when I saw Julie. She was on her haunches, crouched over her blusher compact, reapplying her black eyeliner. She had her weekend coat on—a short white jacket with a belt that pulls in tight at the waist—and her honey-colored suede wedge boots. Even though "behind the science block" means "in that damp, spidery old ditch between the school building and the fence," and even though she was squatting, she looked sophisticated. At least sixteen.

She eyed me up and down. I was wearing my floral summer dress from the Notting Hill Housing Trust, with some warm tartan tights. "Hm," she said, and lurched toward me with her brush in her hand. Before I could move, she'd dabbed my cheeks and, holding my chin firmly, so I couldn't move, applied some of her makeup to my eyes and lips. "Need you to look a bit more conventional," she said. "Bit less odd."

I decided to ignore that and we set off, scrambling over the railings into Hillside Road. We stopped running when we got to Ashcroft Avenue, and leaned, puffing, against a tree. Julie was carrying a big plastic bag and when she'd got her breath back she opened it. Inside were two clipboards. She handed one to me. "Right," she said. "We'll pretend we're doing a project on Shopping Distribution. We're seniors if anyone asks. Okay?"

The shop was empty when we got there. There was no sign of The Pharmacist. Behind the counter was a woman with wiry brown hair, flecked with gray, and pouchy eyes. I wanted to leave—we'd been giggling all the way down and it just felt like a laugh—but Julie marched straight up. "Hello. We're from Woodvale Secondary," she said. "We're doing a school project on the Changing Face of the High Street. Could I speak to the owner, please?"

The woman had been reading *OK!* magazine. She said, "The owner?"

"You know, the bloke who's usually here? In the jeans?"

I cleared my throat. I was thinking about his bum and trying hard not to laugh. Julie jabbed me in the leg with her fingers.

"Oh, John." The woman called through a door beyond the pharmacy section. "Jo-hn. Some girls to see you." To us, she said, "He's developing."

Under my breath I said, "Aren't we all."

Julie nudged me. "How interesting," she said. "Photos. Yes. We must remember—mustn't we, Con? To bring our film here next time we're back from our Club Eighteen to Thirty holiday."

I took in a quick breath and held it. A gust of air blasted out of my nose. Julie put her head on one side and looked at me without blinking. I was working up to make her crack too. I was just by the pregnancy tests. Something wicked was building.

And then he came through the door, and we both turned. First thing: he wasn't wearing jeans. He was pulling off a plastic apron and hanging it on the door and underneath he was all in black: black T-shirt, black trousers, black brows. He was frowning slightly and I suddenly felt rather nervous. He looked nothing like a traveler or an artist and everything like a handsome beetle. Or a rather cross pharmacist.

He came to the counter and Julie, who I could tell was also finding this slightly less funny now because she was gripping my dress between her finger and thumb, ran through her thing again, more nervously this time.

He said, "I see," when she'd finished. "Okay. Fire away."

While she fumbled for her clipboard, he looked at his watch.

I rather thought he might take us out the back or something, but we just stood there, leaning over the Clarins. Julie ran through some questions. How long had he owned the shop? (Six months; he had taken it over from his uncle, Leakey senior.) What was his training? (A five-year course in pharmacology at De Montfort, Leicester.) Was it convenient in terms of locality vis-à-vis his living arrangements? (Yes.) Then she asked him a question about competition within the high street environment. His eyes had been darting around the shop, checking customers, keeping a note on the wire-haired woman's response to them. But now he looked keenly at us and, as Julie had her head down writing, that meant me. His eyes, I noticed, were very dark. I feel cringingly embarrassed remembering this now, because I just stood there with a foolish smile on my face while he talked about sharks and minnows, my head nodding, occasionally glancing at the suppositories to the left of his ear to escape his glare. "So basically, if deregulation goes ahead, it's undercutting on price versus personal service," he concluded. "You're not going to find anyone from the big chains delivering Mrs. Jones's prescription when she can't get out of bed."

Julie looked up. "And where does this Mrs. Jones live? Does she live within the high street environment?"

He frowned.

I cleared my throat. "You're making a general point," I said. "Using a mythical Mrs. Jones as an example. We quite see that, don't we, Julie?"

For a moment Julie looked lost, but then she remembered her notes. "And what about hours?" she said, referring to her clipboard again. "Weekends, some Sundays, late opening, goodness, you were even open on Christmas Day this year, weren't you—how does that work with domestic arrangements?"

He frowned again. "Sorry, is this relevant?" He was looking over our heads. I realized a few people had come into the shop. The assistant with the pouchy eyes had begun serving, but a small line was forming.

"All she means," I added quickly, "is it must dissuade some people from running small businesses, particularly one of this nature. Um—you know, when you're married and have children."

He said, "I suppose so."

Julie said, "So does it?"

He darted a nervous look at the woman with the pouchy eyes. She was bending down at the shelves just behind her—where the things called Benzadrille and Optak are—flicking through them in panic, humming quickly. The Pharmacist—John—said, "I'm sure it would. Now, if you've—"

I suddenly realized that the customer causing the problem was female and very attractive. She was wearing one of those long sheepskin coats that cost about a million pounds, and she was flicking her matching shoulder-length chestnut hair crossly. She looked like a racehorse refusing the water jump.

The Pharmacist Guy moved across. He rested his hand lightly on his assistant's shoulder and asked what the problem was. The racehorse woman took a step back. She muttered something about orange flavor.

The Pharmacist Guy looked at the box on the counter. "I'm afraid Worvex is all we stock. Is it for the whole family?"

The racehorse woman said that no, it was just for her children.

"Hm," he said. "It might be worth you taking a dose yourself. Most adults escape, but you can't be too careful. It can be very . . . irritating." He had bent down and was now holding two packages out toward her. "Best to break the cycle."

The woman was rearing back. She flicked her mane. "I've told *her* I want orange-flavored Threpsen, which is what I've always had before. And I only need one package. I'm sure Boots can help." She turned to go.

Oh dear. And then this thing happened that I can hardly bear to recount. I think I had got caught up in imagining The Pharmacist taking some old lady's tablets around to her, calling through the letter box, "It's only me, Mrs. Jones," being all caring and nice while the big chains ran his business over. I said, really quite loudly, *shamefully* loudly, "Oh, tapeworm, that's a nightmare. We've both had it, haven't we, Julie? And the night itching. God. That's when the female worm exits the anal passage to lay her eggs."

Everybody stared at me, even a gentleman over by the vitamins, even Julie, whose clipboard was now hanging forgotten by her side. But do you know what? After a few agonizing moments, the horsey woman, who had also been staring at me, seemed to sort of weaken—she obviously liked being talked to like that—and she asked me if I really thought Worvex would do, and I told her that actually I thought it would do fine and that my younger brother and sister actually *preferred* the taste of Worvex, as long as you got them to swallow it quickly. "Don't let them suck it," I said. "They kind of explode out if you do." And not only did she then buy one package, she also bought a second—"to be on the safe side." "You want to be on the safe side," I said. "That night itching. It's a killer."

Once the horsey woman had left, all friendly and ponylike now, John gave me a funny look. His eyebrows went up very slightly in the middle. And after that I decided perhaps he wasn't as scary as I'd first thought.

We got out of there finally and walked slowly and maturely down the high street, saying things like, "So that's interesting, isn't it, about the Office of Fair Trading guidelines," and, "Well, Julie, I suppose really we ought to interview the manager of Boots next for a really rounded view," until we got to Chelverton Road, when we ran for a bit, tugging on each other's coats until we were past the bus garage, and then collapsed in a heap of nervous giggles in the gutter. It seemed glorious for a moment to be fourteen, to be so crazy and wicked and find each other so funny. But then Julie had to get home so we got up, dusted ourselves off, and walked to the bus stop. Once there, we ran through What We Had Learned So Far.

A. *He owns the business—which is very good—only it does make his surname Leakey, which has unfortunate incontinent connotations.*

B. *He appears to be single. I was not so sure about this, but Julie said he wouldn't have been so cagey if he had a family. Any excuse, and people with children get out their photos.*

C. *He's nice. Julie wanted to know how I could be sure. I reminded her about the reassuring hand he had put on his assistant's shoulder. Sweet to his staff. Can't say more than that.*

"The only thing is," I said, "if I had to throw one cog in the works, it's quite clear the nature of his job renders him impervious to the charms of the opposite sex."

"What do you mean?"

I drew attention to the fact that our pharmacist hadn't flirted at all, not one iota, not a glimmer, zilch, with the racehorse woman. "And she was attractive," I said. "Very."

Julie said yes, but that she did have tapeworm.

"As far as he's concerned," I pointed out, "everyone has. What our pharmacist sees is the inner ailment. 'Oh, hello, top supermodel: how's the stress incontinence?' Young Hollywood starlet: 'What news on the hemorrhoids?'"

Julie said she thought I was looking for trouble where there wasn't any, but that it was worth covering ourselves. "We've started on The Pharmacist," she said. "Now for Plan B. Watch out, Uncle Bert."

I'm writing this on the loo and I'd better be quick because I've just heard Jack turn up to babysit. I can smell fried fish and he'll be laden with a new bag of pirated videos. Squeals of laughter are coming from downstairs and the occasional bellow from Jack. In a moment there will be a banging on the door. He'll want to know what Mother's up to. She's actually having a drink with her friend Carol, but I won't let on. I'll tell him he's burned his bridges and ask how Jane is. I mean June. I mean Jackie. Oh, sorry, what's the new one called again? And then he'll pretend to box my ears. And the four of us will sit down together, like we used to when he lived here, and watch *Star Wars*, episode five or six or 532 or wherever we're up to. I hope the quality's not too bad; it was quite hard to hear last time. Oh, and then Marie and Cyril will fall into bed, overexcited and tearful. But under the circumstances—viz my appalling attendance record of today—I can't exactly complain.

I've just got one more thing to write. When I got

home after the pharmacy, there was William on the doorstep—*again*. He told me he was locked out, which sounded like an excuse. I was longing to think about today and make plans for Friday—I've told Julie I will go to see the Electric B'stards to suss out Uncle Bert—but I let William in anyway.

We went straight up to the roof, where I was hoping we could sit in companionable silence, but it turned out I was doomed to have my peace shattered because who should stick her curly head out of next-door's window but Delilah, my next-door neighbor.

Delilah is one of those friends you have because of circumstances rather than choice. We've lived next door to each other all our lives—my mother used to babysit her while her mom was at the hairdresser's (about eight times a week)—so I've grown to love her. Well, sort of, anyway. She's going through a funny boy-mad phase and also she's at the girls' high, which is private, so even though we're next-door neighbors (our houses couldn't be more different—hers is like something out of *Elle Decoration*, mine out of *Recycling Weekly*), our lives are miles apart.

This evening she said, "Can you two stop yakking? Some of us have got Latin declensions to do." They do a lot of declenshing at the girls' high.

William said, "What *are* you wearing?" and she darted back in again. I knew what she was doing: getting out of her school gingham pinafore.

I was right. When she came back, she was wearing pinky eyeshadow that clashed with the blueness of her eyes, and a tight white top with cancan dancers prancing across the squishy outline of her padded bra. Delilah's as bad as Mother when it comes to boys. She's even got a Snog Log by her bed.

She said in a mock-Cockney voice she often uses when she talks to William, "So you two coming down the youth club on Friday? They've got a Valentine's Pitch and Putt Special."

William said, "Might." He can be quite laconic when it comes to Delilah.

She said teasingly, "Connie?"

I pretended to think about it for a moment. "Valentine's Day, is it?" I said. I haven't been to the youth club since the summer disco when that boy from north London put his tongue in my throat and I thought I was going to gag. (I do not have a Snog Log and have no intention of *ever getting one*.) I said, "Nah, I'm going to the Electric B'stards."

Delilah and William both looked at me. Delilah was so surprised she forgot to stop sounding fancy. "Really?" (It came out like, "Rilly?')

"Yup. With Julie. Her Uncle Bert gets free tickets."

Delilah said, "On Friday?"

William said, "With Julie?"

They were beginning to annoy me. I know I said I don't go to the youth club, but am I so weird that the thought of me doing anything remotely "teenage" is completely out of the question? I said, "A girl's got to start somewhere."

Delilah was leaning out so far I was worried she might topple, and that would be a shame. She said excitedly, "Ooh, can I do your makeup? What are you going to wear? Hang on." Her curly head disappeared again and then reappeared along with an arm brandishing a magazine. Her voice got all squeaky. She said, "Can I do a Makeover? There's one in here. Look at her there, before, and then look at her after. Oh, go on, Con. I've always wanted to do a Makeover." She gave me one of her appealing gap-toothed smiles.

I became all dignified then and told her that I was happy as I was. William, laughing, said the polyester dress and thick stockings look was greatly underrated, so I had to dig him in the ribs.

He did lots of "Ow"ing and schoolboy doubling up, all feet and limbs.

Before she poked her head back in, Delilah said prettily, "See you on Friday, then, Will."

Will? Who does she think she is?

Chapter Four

SATURDAY, FEBRUARY 15 *(or the morning after the Electric B'stards)* *11:30 a.m.*

It's a boisterous day—the glass in the back door is rattling and birds are wheeling high up in the white sky. We've just been to confession. It's ironic but true that when I last wrote in here—four days ago—I felt gloriously wicked. Now I'm deep in sin.

I did confess something. I said how furious and resentful I felt yesterday when everyone was bandying their French-exchange letters about. I asked Father O'Connor whether I wasn't too young for self-sacrifice and he said, "My child, you are never too young to do what the good Lord wants." So then I was in a bad mood and didn't confess any of the things I should have.

Confession No. 1: Unkind Words

The first thing I should have confessed to was my reaction yesterday morning to William's valentine card. I should have thanked him nicely and left it at that. He stood rubbing the back of his neck while I opened it. I knew what it was going to be. Our house that morning was no stranger to the valentine card. Mother had two (*Two!* One from Jack, but the other?), and Marie has been busy with the glitter for weeks now.

William said, "Is it okay?"

It was quite plain as cards go: pink flowers on the outside and "Love?" in pink bubble-writing within. Technically it was my first ever. I got sent one a few years ago, but it turned out to be from Mother. (Note to self: never, unless you are into ritual humiliation, send a valentine card to your own daughter.)

"Yeah," I said lightly.

"I bought it just now," he said.

I told him I could tell because the glue on the envelope was still damp. I yanked my bike out past him and said, "But you didn't have to."

And then a goofy expression came over his face, like he was expecting something more from me.

"Come on," I said. "Race you."

"Okay," he said. "Girly from the block."

"What?"

Well, I won't bore on. But basically it turned out *he'd* got a valentine card himself that—*duh*—he thought was from me. Would I ever call myself "girly from the block'? I ask you. He pulled the card in question out of his pocket—if I *had* sent it, I might have wanted to have words about how scrumpled it was—and one look at the handwriting and I knew which blue-eyed pink-eye-shadowed "girly from the block" it was from.

"That's not from me. That's from Delilah," I said. I held the card he'd sent *me* out to *him* and said, "Give it to her, then. I don't want it."

William had been laughing—not at all embarrassed like he should have been—but at this he flushed. He got on his bike and rode off. I biked after him but I didn't catch up with him. Time was when I won any race, but recently he seems to be outpacing me. Still, at least I've still got an inch on him in height.

I met Delilah in the street later. In honor of the Valentine's Day Pitch and Putt, she was wearing a T-shirt with lipstick kisses all over it and had painted a red heart on each cheek.

"Big on hearts today, aren't you?" I said.

She smiled coyly. "Did Will tell you about the card, then? What did he say?"

I hesitated and then said he was quite pleased.

She smiled again, her cheek hearts bunching. "I sent ten," she said.

I said I hadn't realized she *knew* ten boys.

She sniffed. "Don't forget I was in the school play. We borrowed boys for that."

Confession No. 2: Deceiving Others

At school Julie was clutching two valentine cards. They were both the size of billboards with padded velvet hearts in the center. Inside of each was printed: "Roses are red / Violets are blue / My heart's all furry / Stroke it, please do."

One, she said, was from Mother to The Pharmacist, the other from Mother to Mr. Baker. There was no point sending one to Uncle Bert, as Mother hadn't met him yet.

I said, "I'm not sending a card to Mr. Baker."

She tried to persuade me, but I wouldn't be budged.

"Oh, all right, then," she said, running her tongue over her sumptuous lips. "But The Pharmacist? Okay? You've got to do it because you know your mom's handwriting."

"All right," I said.

"And you've got to think of something she buys there that he might know her by."

"Like what?"

"I dunno. Toothpaste? Lipstick?"

I racked my brain. Mother hadn't been in for months. Not since Marie had that weird rash. There was only one thing she bought regularly. . . .

"Okay. I know," I said.

We did it in break and I dropped it in on my way home. Luckily, the woman with the wiry hair didn't see me. There was a new poster in the window saying AID NOT BOMBS and a small notice next to it, advertising a vacancy. I slipped the card through the letter box.

What he's going to think when he sees it, I don't know. The card read, "All my love from the satisfied purchaser of Neutrogena T/Gel Anti-Dandruff Shampoo."

Confessions Nos. 3, 4, 5: Appropriation of Another's Property, Inconsideration Toward Fellow Human Beings, Total Lack of Compassion, or Just General Wickedness
Which brings me to last night, Uncle Bert, and the Electric B'Stards.

Julie, who seems to be having more fun with this than I could have thought imaginable—really, she's wasted at school, I've told her that—said I had only one job when she and Uncle Bert came to pick me up, and that was not to come down after I heard the doorbell. I was to wait upstairs, pretending to get ready, for *thirty minutes*. She needed the time, she said, a) to give Mother and Bert a chance to get to know each other, and b) to plant her props. Her plan was to steal his phone and hide it some-where in our house. I was to "find' it the next day and then he'd have to come by to collect it.

Naturally I didn't need the extra time to get ready. I hate looking at myself in the mirror. There are all these bulges these days that don't seem to meld together like they should. I know I should have a proper bra—not just an undershirt—but I don't like drawing attention to my boobs. I'd rather they were hidden away. They're nowhere near as big as Julie's anyway. And I already knew what I was going to wear: what I was wearing already (which happened to be the knee-length tweed skirt and purple polyester top I'd worn to school).

So when Julie, Uncle Bert, and Sue, his girlfriend, were drawing up outside our house, I was just sitting in the bathroom, waiting. I missed the next bit, but Julie told me about it later.

Apparently Bert didn't switch the engine off, just told Julie to run in and get me. He's "in merchandising," you see, and needed to get back to the venue "sharpish." Julie, thinking fast, put on a little girl's voice: "Oh, but it's so dark." Uncle Bert, impatient to get the show on the road (literally), switched off the ignition, got out, and came to the door with her—leaving Sue in the car. (God, Julie was pleased with herself when she told me this.)

All I heard was Mother calling, "Constance! Time, time, time!"

"Just doing my hair," I yelled back. "Give me five minutes. Sorry."

Downstairs, Uncle Bert huffed a bit, but Mother told them to come in and they stood in the kitchen while she cleared the dishes. She'd taken her eyes out because they were hurting and I knew she was wearing her big black-rimmed glasses. By now she had also stepped out of her heels and was tiptoeing around the kitchen in her tights. Julie said this wasn't a problem, that it made her seem even more petite (in a completely unrelated aside, can I point out how uncomfortable it is being so much *bigger* than one's mother?), which was lucky because Uncle Bert is quite small himself.

Unfortunately Mother's charm was not in full flow. For one thing, she kept coming to the bottom of the stairs and calling up. Julie said Uncle Bert looked at his watch and jigged about, but some sort of conversation struggled through. Mother said it was very kind of him to take me—"if Constance ever, ever, ever appears!"—and he said it was a pleasure, that it was nice to let others enjoy the perks of his job. Silence. He studied the photograph of Euston Road in the rain that we have on the wall. He said, "Is it New York?" and Mother said, "No, it's 'uston Road." He said, "Houston? In Texas?" And she said, "No, 'uston Road in 'uston, London." Unlucky this: she gets annoyed when people pick up on her accent. (She thinks she doesn't have one.)

For me, upstairs, waiting the first ten minutes wasn't too bad. Then I began to worry. It's my worst sort of thing, not doing what's expected of you. I paced for a bit, and then I sat on the stool, listening to the leaking bath tap *drip, drip, drip*. Each time Mother called up, my heart gave a leap of anxiety. Then I began to pick at the stool's cork top. I studied the stain on the bath until I made it look like a wizard with a huge gold cloak. And then a strange thing happened. I began to think I would sit there forever. I would just sit there picking at the stool all night. My watch ticked around to seven o'clock and for a few seconds I stared at it, wondering what I was supposed to do now.

Then I heard Julie shout, "Constance. We're ready for you!" and I jumped to it.

When I came down, all I could smell was cKone. Mother looked at my hair, which I'd just pulled back, and said, *"Chérie!"* rather weakly. Julie snorted. (What were they expecting? A Mohawk?) Uncle Bert didn't say anything. He was already halfway out of the door. Julie gave me a thumbs-up behind his back to show she'd done the deed. Mother kissed me, smudging with her thumb a little bit of what I assumed to be toothpaste away from the side of my mouth, and told us to amuse ourselves.

In the car there was "an atmosphere." I don't think Uncle Bert's girlfriend had appreciated being kept waiting. She was squashed up in the back with me and I kept saying I was sorry, but her annoyance didn't seem to be directed at me. There was a sports bag gaping open between us with a white T-shirt bundled in at the top, half hanging out. It smelled of Bert's cKone and she kept twisting it with one hand and punching it farther in.

Uncle Bert's car, according to Julie, is a Spider, but it felt more like a Fly in the back: zippy, still, and then fast with sudden spurts of acceleration. Something was buzzing, too: I think it might have been a vibration in the window frames. All the way to Hammersmith, Julie would twist around from the front seat and say things like, "So *how* old was your mother when she had you? . . . So young." "A widow at twenty-three! How did your father die? Killed delivering pizzas? That's so sad. So brave. Brave as well as beautiful." "Bernadette. That is *such* a romantic name."

I couldn't help laughing out loud at that one, but most of the time I was more worried about Sue. It may just have been the position she was in—her knees bent around to one side, her blond head slightly ducked—but she seemed to have lost some of her karmic poise. She's very pretty, despite the length of her hair.

In the noisy, buzzy bits of the journey, when Julie wasn't talking, Sue told me she did corporate entertaining—that's how she met Bert. "I meet a lot of men in my line of work," she said. She lives in Stockwell and grew up in south Wales. She doesn't normally go to this sort of gig with Bert but, because it was Valentine's Day, she had made an exception. Also she was going to Australia for three weeks for her sister's wedding, so she wasn't going to see him for a bit. She said I asked a lot of questions and could she ask me one herself? "How come you and Julie are friends?" she said, scrutinizing me. "You seem so . . ."

"Grown-up," I finished for her. "Yes, a lot of people say that."

When we got to the venue, Bert had to go off and do something, and he told us a good place to wait for him, which was to one side of the stage. It was dark, and smelled of stale spilled beer and sweat. When Sue went to get us some Cokes, Julie filled me in on everything that had happened when I was in the bathroom, including the whole "'uston" photograph thing. When Sue came back, I noticed they were both in combats. Julie's were army and baggy, down by her navel, while Sue's were satiny and tight. Julie lit up a cigarette then, which was interesting. She wouldn't do it in front of her uncle, but she did in front of Sue, as if to let her know it didn't count. Oh, and then it got busier and busier and Bert appeared, also,

I now realized, in combats (the whole *place* was in combats), and steered us to the middle, and the noise level began to rise and everyone was shouting and the Electric B'stards started playing and I felt squeezed on every side.

I wish I could say I loved the Electric B'stards. It would be nice to shepherd in the rebellious teenage years of Connie Pickles. Julie's face was raised and her eyes were sparkling with excitement—it got so hot, her hair was sticking to her face—but I . . . I just kept feeling these irresistible yawns beginning at my jaw. Isn't that awful? And, after a while, I slipped to the back, where it was cooler and where the crowd was much looser, and found a seat that no one was sitting on and took out the book that I'd smuggled into the pocket of my jacket. I'm still reading *The Blessing*. I've got to the part where Sigi, the only child of Grace and Charles-Edouard, has managed to split up his parents. I've just realized he does the opposite to me—he's an anti-matchmaker, I'm a matchmaker.

Afterward we went for fish and chips on the Fulham Palace Road. Uncle Bert seemed more relaxed once the gig was over. He has a handsome face and longish blond hair that he tosses a lot, but a rather scraggy neck. He gave us T-shirts with "Electric B'stards" written across the back, and we put them on over what we were wearing. Sue seemed jolly too, though I did feel sorry for her sitting in a fish and chip shop with two teenage girls on

Valentine's Night. Uncle Bert didn't do the thing with her waistband. No candlelight, either. In fact, the glaring neon bouncing off the Formica table made her look tired. She was next to me and there was a yellowy dried powder over her face and spots of mascara like tiny, trapped flies in the corners of her eyes. She didn't look so pretty after all, which made me feel guiltier about what we were doing to her. Particularly as Julie was ignoring her. I kept having to remind myself of Mother, who didn't meet a lot of men in *her* line of work.

I wasn't eating because when Bert asked if I was hungry, I'd been too polite to say yes, and then it would have been too embarrassing to change my mind. I watched Julie's mouth crunching on delicious crispy batter. She asked me several more pointed questions about Mother and I tried to answer truthfully, but without slipping from The Plan. We had already discussed how important it was to bring out Uncle Bert's protective instinct to make up for the fact that Mother was saddled with three children. I told them about the leaking tap in the bathroom and the water that comes in through the flat roof on wet nights and Mother's long hours at work. Julie had been insistent that Uncle Bert discover the nature of Mother's employment. She said she thought all men were tickled by the idea of fancy underwear. And actually it did seem to stir his interest. He'd just been jogging his knees and doing pretend-drum rolls on the table before then. "Belgravia?" he said. "Very exclusive. And does she model what she sells?" Sue said, "Oh, I should pop in one day. I've always wanted to be measured," and Julie gave her a withering look. It's true that Sue (like me) is quite flat up top. Then Julie froze her face into a small, bored smile and looked away. I know she was dissing her for Mother's sake, but I wonder whether she wasn't also doing it a bit for her own sake too.

Uncle Bert wanted to give Julie's mom a call to say we were leaving, but when he felt in his jacket, he couldn't find his phone! "Oh my God, I must have dropped it!" he said.

Julie, her eyes as wide as saucers, said she was sure she'd felt it jabbing into her when they were squashed up at the gig.

"It must have fallen out of my pocket, or been stolen," he said. He looked at his watch (one of those enormous diving watches). "The Palais'll be closed now. I'll have to go back tomorrow. Bugger it." He frowned, his good mood wiped away.

When we got in the car Julie squeezed my leg. "'Find' it tomorrow," she whispered.

So, here I am now, surrounded by the pure, wiped-clean souls that make up my family. Cyril is busy with his Flags of the World jigsaw. Marie is preening her Barbie Head. Mother is in the garden, in a fetching white T-shirt and cut-off jeans, tackling weeds. Even the cat, skittish because of the wind, is charging in and out of the house as if he didn't have a care in the world. An innocent pharmacist is baffling over his valentine card. And I'm sitting at the kitchen counter, up to my neck in sin.

In front of me is Uncle Bert's Nokia. And a Fly that thinks it's a Spider is buzzing through the south London streets toward our web.

⅋

The kitchen counter, five minutes later

Well, now I feel a total idiot.

He came. He saw. He took his mobile phone. He left.

I've just rung Julie on *her* mobile phone. She was shopping in New Look.

"'uston," I said. "We 'ave a problem."

"Hang on. Let me get out to the sidewalk. What do you mean?"

"He didn't stay," I told her.

"What do you mean, he didn't stay?"

"He left the engine running."

"Where was Bernadette?"

"In the garden."

"Couldn't you have called her?"

"Julie. He was blocking the road. He left the car door open."

She sighed very heavily. Julie takes disappointment hard. "After all that," she said.

"I know. I'm sorry."

She sighed again. "Well, listen. Uncle Bert's coming around later. Sue's left for Australia, so he's on his own. He always comes around to our house for his meals when he's on his own. He's probably on his way now. Leave it with me. I'll think of something. I'm bored stiff today. I'll ring you later. Okay? Don't do anything. Don't go anywhere. Don't move."

"There's still The Pharmacist," I said weakly. But she'd hung up.

So much for all that sin. Turns out we didn't achieve anything to be ashamed of at all. How shaming is that?

I think I'll take Marie and Cyril to the park to absolve *intention* to sin, and rudeness to William, and all the other things that are weighing on my soul. I might even, as we're passing, see if there's anything new in Cancer Research.

&

STILL SATURDAY
5 p.m.

There was. A dark-blue silk jacket from Agnès b.— threadbare but French!—and a pair of pink OshKosh dungarees that are perfect for Marie. (She only really wears pink.) Cyril set his heart on a light in the shape of the globe, but it wasn't working and cost the earth.

At the swings Cyril saw some boys from school and I tried to make him go up and play soccer with them, but he said he wanted to stay with us. Marie held my hand, and we sat on the bench together and had one of those impromptu bonding conversations about burial versus cremation. She said, "Jesus was buried, but when they rolled back the stone, he had got up again, hadn't he? Did he get cremated then?"

Cyril said, "No, silly. He lived forever and ever. For eternity."

Marie looked at us both. "Whoa," she said simply.

On the way home we went by the pharmacy. I thought I'd buy some Neutrogena T/Gel Anti-Dandruff Shampoo as we were passing. As a hint. On the way in, I saw again the ad for a vacancy. It read: "VACANCY. Reliable Assistant, Saturdays Only. Inquire within." *A Saturday girl!* Money. Proximity to our prey. It was like a lightbulb going on above my head. I'd failed with Bert, but here was my chance to redeem myself with Julie.

John Leakey was at the register. The shop was empty. I didn't really know I was going to say it until I did.

I said, "Some Neutrogena T/Gel Anti-Dandruff

Shampoo for my mother, please. And, um . . . are you looking for someone for Saturdays?"

He looked up from his paper. "Hello. You're the worm girl."

"I saw the ad. I just wondered."

Marie was spinning around the display of hair grips. Cyril was standing by my side.

"Hm," The Pharmacist said. "We are actually. Are you interested?"

"Yes."

"And you're sixteen?"

I hesitated. "Yes."

"And do you have any retail experience?"

"No. But I'm eager to learn."

He considered me for a moment. "And will you be willing to share with the customers your experience of night itching?"

"Absolutely," I said. "If that's what's needed."

He gave a shout of a laugh. And when we walked out five minutes later, he'd given me a tryout for next week. I made us all run down the street. He is offering five pounds an hour. Eight hours a day. Eight times five equals forty. Forty pounds a week! What we could all do with that! I couldn't wait to get home and tell Mother. And ring Julie.

I forgot all about it when I reached the house. Jack's van was parked outside, and inside I could hear banging in the bathroom. He must be trying to mend the leaking tap. Delilah had dropped in to tell me all about the youth club's Valentine's Night and hadn't yet found her way home, and . . . next to each other on the sofa, facing Mother and Delilah, were Julie and Uncle Bert.

I stood there in the doorway, The Pharmacist forgotten. Uncle Bert was looking serious and Julie—Julie's face bore the signs of recent tumultuous tears, which is to say streaked blue mascara and swollen lips.

Mother leaped to her feet when she saw me. "Constance!" she shrieked. "Your poor friend . . . How could you be so t'oughtless?"

"What?" I said. "What?"

Julie sniffed. "It's all right," she mumbled into her sleeve.

"What's happened?" I said.

Uncle Bert stood up, rearranging his jeans. "It's cool," he said. "No worries. You're here now. Safe and sound. All right, chickacheet?" he said to Julie.

She nodded, looking down at the floor.

"What's happened?" I said again. But I knew it was a scam now. Julie never looks at the floor in case she misses anything.

Everyone glared at me as if I were the Devil Incarnate. Typical. When I had begun to think my sins were absolved. I even heard Delilah tut. (But then she doesn't like Julie, so that could have meant anything.)

"Go on," I said.

This is her story. She said she'd been due to meet me in the King's Road at 2 p.m. When I didn't show up, she was stuck because the night before she'd given me her purse to look after and I hadn't given it back. She only had enough money to get there, not enough to go home. She kept ringing me, but our phone was engaged, so finally she'd rung her mom, and Uncle Bert, who was in her kitchen having lunch, agreed to come and pick her up. She'd been so worried about her purse and her dear missing friend Constance that he said he'd bring her around to my house to see me for herself. And then I wasn't in (Julie took her eyes off the floor to glare at me), but my kind, kind, beautiful mother had made them some tea.

My kind, kind, beautiful mother said, "Constance. I am appalled at you."

"I forgot," I said.

It was a shame Delilah was there because when Julie came upstairs "to get her purse," she trotted up too and we couldn't really talk. I made a ridiculous kerfuffle about stuffing nothing in Julie's back pocket and promising never to be so t'oughtless again. I told them both about the tryout at the drugstore—Julie said "good girl"—and then the two of them exchanged spiky sort of competitive words about who had had the nicest Friday night. I don't know why they don't like each other; I suppose they're so different. Julie said the Electric B'stards were mind-blowing. Delilah said Pitch and Putt had been "like, a total riot," that she had been "like, totally wasted."

I asked if William had gone. She said, laughing privately to herself, "Yeah, yeah, yeah. The boys were all just, like, totally mad and put the girls' balls down their trousers."

"*Très amusant,*" said I.

Delilah went to the loo and Julie and I managed to have a quick confab. I felt a bit cross about being in trouble with everyone, but I had to admire her ingenuity. In the car over, she'd told Bert that Mother was very fussy about men.

"Fussy?" I said.

"You know, thrill of the chase and all that," she replied.

When we got downstairs again, Mother and Uncle Bert were sitting quite close to each other, but they were only talking about the congestion charge. Jack, who's a big man with a lot of hair, was standing in the doorway, looking fat, proprietorial, and fishy—literally and metaphorically. Marie and Cyril were bouncing around trying to get Jack's attention, but it was the other conversation Jack was trying to get in on. "Yep," he kept saying, on a sniff. "Yep. It's small businesses like mine you have to worry about."

Something about the presence of Jack seemed to make Uncle Bert particularly charming. He was looking at Mother in a funny way. His eyes seemed to be focused on her hair. They got on to the French language. He'd always meant to learn. He'd love to live in Paris one day (sharp intake of breath from me). That lovely French food. He asked if she'd tried Chez Pierre in the high street. "Once," she said. "But it would be so, so, so nice to go again."

Beyond them in the garden, I could see that the fork she had dug into the earth when she'd been gardening earlier had fallen backward. Prongs up, it looked lethal, like a trap.

Julie and Uncle Bert had to get back. I did lots of apologizing at the door—to Julie and to Uncle Bert for putting him out—so we were still standing there when Mr. Spence jogged up. God, that man gets everywhere. Mother smiled vaguely at him, her hand half raised as if to say "just a minute." She seemed to beam all the more shinily at Uncle Bert, telling him he was "a ver', ver', ver' kind man." Uncle Bert got all brisk and just said, "Any time."

As they drove off, Julie put her face to the passenger window and waved. There was some new ingredient in the smile she gave me. Oh, I know: pure wickedness.

Chapter Five

1 p.m.

Back from church and the phone's just rung. Mother's taken it into the garden, which is suspicious. I can hear her giggling. Very Interesting.

§

1:10 p.m.

"Who was that?" I just asked her.

"No one," she said. "No one important."

§

1:45 p.m.

William's been around. He still hasn't found his hamster. He said his dad's probably drunk it.

"How was the Pitch and Putt?" I asked. "I hear you stuffed your balls down the girls' trousers?" Apparently,

I'd got it wrong. They'd been stuffing the girls' balls down their own trousers. "I see," I said. "An altogether more sophisticated soirée."

"You," he said, tweaking up his hair in the mirror above my bed, "can bugger right off." I could smell something floral, like he's started using gel.

I've just rung Julie. She said Uncle Bert asked her questions about Mother all the way home.

§

2 p.m.

Mother has moved the chair into the middle of the sitting room, so she can see her reflection in the mirror. She's trying on clothes.

She's run herself a bath. It's not even three o'clock in the afternoon.

§

6:30 p.m.

Jack's come around to babysit. "I didn't know Mother was going out?" I said.

"Nor did I," he answered.

The house smells of rose and geranium.

§

7 p.m.

Mother has vacated the building. She says she's meeting her friend Carol. I don't believe her. I said, "Mother. I need to know where you are going. For security reasons."

She laughed. "I won't be late," she said. "It's not far."

"Where isn't?" I said.

"Chez Pierre," she said. "In the high street."

⅌

11:30 p.m.

I fell asleep. I meant to stay awake to see who dropped her home. The house is dark and silent. I'll tiptoe down to see if I can find any evidence.

⅌

11:33 p.m.

I'm back. Mother's asleep—alone—on the sofa bed. There are no coffee mugs, no long blond hairs. But her jacket's on the banister and you couldn't miss it. The sweet, unmistakable smell of cKone.

Chapter Six

FRIDAY, FEBRUARY 21
The bathroom

Julie and I, the cleverest fourteen-year-olds on the planet, have pulled off the matchmake of the century. In one week. Her uncle—the interestingly scented Bert—is going out with my mother. Sorted. Dealt with. Done.

They say it's just French lessons. Yeah, right.

So why am I not happy? Why aren't I cracking open the champagne bottles and dusting off my passport?

I can't put my finger on it. It's less than a week since Mother and Uncle Bert went to Chez Pierre, so it's early days. It's not like they're getting married tomorrow or anything. I just feel guilty. This evening when she was getting ready Mother seemed so excited—she'd bought a new sweater specially—and I felt rather sheepish, as if I'd been cheating in an exam.

William doesn't help. He was here when Uncle Bert

picked her up, and after they'd gone he asked me how on earth they'd met. I told him about Bert's phone and Julie's purse and he said gnomishly, "It must be fate." I felt so grubby I had to go and wash my hands.

Also I keep remembering Sue punching Uncle Bert's cKone-infused gym bag. I'm hoping she's having a nice time in Australia. But she did say she met a lot of men in her work, didn't she? So maybe she'll meet another one soon.

I must try and forget all that. The good thing is it does seem to be going well.

On Monday at breakfast I asked Mother straight if it was Uncle Bert she'd been out with the night before. (Must stop calling him Uncle Bert. It makes him sound like some dodgy entertainer with a rabbit in his pocket.) She went a bit pink and said, "Yes, yes. He's a bit lonely and his stomach was empty. I said I would give him some French lessons. It would be a big, big, big help with his merchandising."

So he came around on Tuesday and she made him supper (*crêpe à la fromage*; a bit like cheese on toast only fancier) and they sat at the kitchen counter, knee to knee, sipping wine and giggling over his schoolboy pronunciation. And then he came again on Wednesday (cheese soufflé: ditto). And tonight they've gone to see a French film in town, "to perfect his accent."

It's all ver', ver', ver'—as Mother would say—exciting. Julie high-fives me at school every day. On Monday she said, "That'll teach her," and I wasn't quite sure what she meant until I realized she was referring to Sue. She really doesn't like her. I told her we might be cousins soon, which she didn't understand at first and then she laughed. "God," she said. "Yeah. I s'pose." There's been lots of talk at school this week about the approaching war. People were handing out leaflets at the gates. The news is full of it. There's going to be a march next week. I think Julie's mind's on that. As mine should be too.

Anyway, I must have an early night. That's another thing to record. It's my first day at the drugstore tomorrow. I'm feeling calm and collected about it. Completely in control. Aghghghg.

Chapter Seven

SATURDAY, FEBRUARY 22
My bedroom, 6 p.m.

I'm a natural! John—Mr. Leakey to you!—said so. He said, "Well, Connie, you have a way with customers, I must say. You ask the right questions and you know when to shut up. That was a good day's work. Thank you."

Mostly I just have to stack shelves and flash around the price gun. I'm allowed to serve, but I'm not allowed to handle drugs. I told John that's fine. If anyone asks, I'll just say no.

Gail—that's the woman with the pouchy eyes and wiry hair—said she liked my sweater. I told her it was from Oxfam and she breathed in sharply. "Oh," she said. "Looks like cashmere from Harrods." I can tell we're going to be friends.

John wasn't there the whole time. He had errands to

run. I'm still a bit shy of him, but it was nicer when he was around.

It wasn't very busy. Granny Enid pottered in to buy indigestion tablets to spy on me, and that was a bit embarrassing. She'd had her beehive newly done. "I hope you're behaving yourself, young lady," she said, and I wanted to duck under the counter. (She's Jack's mom, so she's not actually my grandmother, but she treats me as if she is.) Later there was a whole surge of underage boys hulking over the mint-flavored condoms, which I found rather challenging. Otherwise it was mainly shampoo and toothpaste and old dears and their prescriptions. During one lull John asked me to give the door a little wipe down and the AID NOT BOMBS poster fell off. We had a proper conversation then. I told him our school was planning a march and he said good for us. He said he thinks it's great that young people are aware of the world outside and engage with it. Think globally, act locally. He said the government should listen to its people, that if the kids are shaking off their apathy to campaign against this war—it might be in a far-off place, but it impacts morally on all of us—it should tell them something important about the strength of feeling in the country as a whole.

I nodded a lot and resolved then and there to shake off my own apathy. And to find out more about the war. (Note to self: Watch news.)

He isn't as scary as you think. He listens to you when you talk and gives a succession of thoughtful little nods when you've finished. His eyes are so dark they are almost black. Maybe he has Italian blood: I should ask him. I wonder if he ever got our/Mother's valentine card. I sneaked a look under the register, but it wasn't there. He must have taken it home.

He paid me in cash and I gave it straight to Mother when I came in. She was very sweet and wouldn't take it. I wouldn't *keep* it, so we had a little spat. In the end, she put it in the empty cookie jar on the shelf in the kitchen. Sort of no-man's-land. She said she hopes I won't end up a simple shopgirl like her. I gave her a hug and told her she's much more than a simple shopgirl. She's a lingerie artiste.

ℬ

10:30 p.m.

I broke off the above because actual, not imminent, war seemed to be breaking out somewhere below me in our house. Screaming, shouting, thumping: all hell, etc. I rushed downstairs to find Marie having a major tantrum in the front room. She was clinging on to Mother's waist, her face contorted, screaming, "Don't leave me. Don't leave me." She was wearing a glittery tiara and a pink nylon party dress. A princess, only a demonic one.

Jack was sitting on the sofa and Bert was standing in the doorway looking panicked. Cyril was in the middle of them all, watching TV as if nothing was happening.

Mother was trying to extricate Marie's fingers while cooing, "*Chérie, chérie* . . . Bert just needs his lesson. I will not be late. Papa is here."

"I'm here," said Jack. "Come on, sweetie, come to Daddy."

Bert said, "Right, well. Better be off, hadn't we?"

Marie started screaming again. "I want to come. I want to come. It's *not fair*. You're always leaving me. Every night, you're leaving me."

Mother sat down on the floor. I could tell Marie had won then. So could Marie. She started whimpering. "Can't we come, Mama? Can't we all come?"

Mother looked at Bert. Bert tried to look away. But failed. He looked nervous.

"We're just going for a Chinese," Mother said. "You don't like Chinese."

Marie scrambled to her feet. "I do. I do. I love it."

So we all went. I don't know quite how it happened. But it did. Mother, Uncle Bert, Jack, Cyril, Marie, and *moi*. We all went to Uncle Bert's favorite Chinese restaurant to thank Mother for the week of French lessons. We went in Jack's van because it could fit us, so now we all smell of fish. Poor Jack. I noticed he ended up paying, too.

It was perfectly pleasant. It wasn't Uncle Bert's fault that our food took so long in coming that Marie—who'd been overtired all along; am I the only person with enough sense to have realized that?—fell asleep in her Singapore noodles. And I do think Uncle Bert could have made it clearer to Cyril that the Kung-Po Special was squid-related, but maybe he thought we went for a Chinese all the time. Jack and he got a bit funny over the wine list, too. There was a sort of tussle. Jack began to say something about the house red, but Bert overrode him. He grabbed the menu and said, "Oh no, not Côtes du Rhône. I only drink New World. French wine is so overrated."

I just think it was a bit tactless, that's all. It was as if he forgot himself for a moment there, as if he'd just been pretending before.

Chapter Eight

Sunday, February 23
Delilah's very grown-up bedroom, 2 p.m.

I bumped into Delilah on the way back from church and she made me come to her house for lunch. She was so bored she wanted to kill herself, she said. Not the most enticing invitation in the world. But I came anyway. I needed cheering up. The thing is, I rang Julie earlier to tell her about the Chinese.

She said, "You went to a Chinese? The one by the river? He took you to his favorite Chinese?" Like she didn't quite believe me. "All of you?"

There was something in her voice that made me think she wasn't happy about it. I tried to make her laugh by telling her about the Kung-Po Special, but she said she had to go before I'd finished. "What a big happy family," she said before she hung up. But not *nicely*.

I hope she's all right. I hope I haven't done something to upset her.

You can never upset Delilah. Not even if you try. She's so thick-skinned it's hilarious. We're wearing orange-and-oatmeal face packs at the moment, so we can't talk because of cracks. That's why I'm writing in here. She is filling in her Snog Log. She's got quite a lot of filling in to do. William, who was at Mass this morning, looking lanky in his trendy trousers, told me he'd seen her at a club in Richmond last night, "high as a kite." I mentioned this as soon as I got here, thinking she'd be sheepish. Fat chance. "I was just, like, wasted," she said. Apparently she got off with a boy. "I think it was *a* boy," she added. "It might have been two."

She's been on at me all morning. She can't believe I don't wear a proper bra. She says I've got good legs even if my hips are wide and that my elegant eyes show that I'm trustworthy and good at keeping secrets. She read all that from one of her magazines. There was more to say about the rest of me, but I crossed my arms and told her to get off my back—not to mention my earlobes and my cheekbones. I hate thinking about my body, let alone discussing it.

"Best friend or lover?" she started on after that. "Have you entered the Boy Danger Zone?"

"The what?" I said.

It was some quiz in the magazine. It claimed you

couldn't be friends with a boy without sexual tension. Delilah said I had to like William because everybody else does. I had to explain what it's like in the real world— i.e., among normal people who don't wear blazers and gingham dresses on a daily basis. In the real world no one likes William. "You lot," I said, "are just desperate." That shut her up.

Oh, her mom's called us down for lunch. Time to take off our face packs. I do hope I haven't got a rash.

$\mathscr{E}$

My very ungrown-up bedroom, 3 p.m.

I've got a rash. But at least I'm home. Lunch at Delilah's can be a bit much. It's not just the smartness and the neatness around there—their house is extended in every possible direction and modern and all painted white—it's the tension zigzagging in the air. Mother might be hopeless, but at least she doesn't try to "understand adolescence" like Marcus and Tanya.

Marcus, who works in the City, flashed his napkin on to his lap and said, "So, Connie, it's a hard year at school this one, isn't it? All those hormones and a heavy workload. Though your mother tells me you're doing brilliantly at Woodvale."

"Clever girl," added Tanya, smiling at me. I saw Marcus give her a look over the wooden and cloth sculpture in the middle of the table (a Madagascan fertility symbol, apparently). It meant: "And here we are spending all this money on school fees."

Delilah knew what it meant too. She said, "So why can't I go to Woodvale, then? I hate the high school. It's all girls. It's not the real world. I'm never going to meet any proper boys." By that I suppose she meant properly meet any boys as opposed to just snogging them in the dark.

Marcus cleared his throat. "I know, darling. I do understand. Maybe we'll think about it after finals." If I hadn't been there, I expect he'd have said something about the kind of proper boy she'd meet at Woodvale. If I ever bump into him or Tanya when I'm with William, they look at him as if there might be something nasty on the bottom of his shoes.

Then we started talking about the imminent war. Marcus and Tanya are all for it. They said things like "enough is enough" and "people have got to learn to see sense." What did I think? I told them about the march planned at school.

Marcus tutted. "Kids," he said. "It's just knee-jerk. There are complications in the situation that are beyond them."

I wanted to say some of the things John Leakey had

said—think globally, act locally—but I wasn't sure it was the moment. I suspect Marcus takes his understanding of adolescence only so far. Anyway, Delilah got there first. She'll use any excuse to go from mild parental resentment to full parental hatred.

"You're just a fascist," she said, jumping down from the table and storming out. "I hate you."

See what I mean. Quite tense.

I went upstairs to see her when I'd finished my plate of food. She was lying on her new platform bed (very grown-up), under her pop posters (very grown-up), hugging Floppy Bunny (not very grown-up). We had a general moan about parents—Marcus and Tanya are going away in a few weeks' time and she says they won't let her have a party, but she's going to have one anyway—and I ended up telling her about the Woodvale march. She looked positively thrilled. We can go to war, she said, but not in her name. She says she's going to blow off her netball match to join it. "That'll show Dad," she said.

I said I was probably going to go too and we tentatively arranged to meet at the real estate agent's at the top of the high street. "But, Delilah," I said, "I doubt the environment will be conducive to meeting boys."

"There are times," she answered, "when one's personal life has to go on the back burner."

"I'm glad you think that," I said. "People might be about to die, after all."

"Exactly," she said. "Got time for a pedicure before you go?"

Chapter Nine

MONDAY, FEBRUARY 24
At home, 5 p.m.

oom and damnation. Something is up with Julie. Definitely. I saw her talking to Carmen at break. They were sitting on the radiators. When I went up, she hardly registered my presence. Finally, she said, "Enjoy the egg rolls, then?"

"Yes, they're delicious, aren't they?" I felt like a puppy trying to lick her hand. But she just gave a chilly laugh and turned back to Carmen. In the end I walked off.

I saw Carmen as I was going through the gates later and asked her if she knew what was up. She said that I should know and that if I didn't I wasn't the friend I thought I was. So now I'm really confused. I don't know whether to be upset or angry.

Mother's home and full of good spirits. She's bought some fancy bacon—pancetta—from the Italian delicatessen near the lingerie shop and so there's spaghetti carbonara for supper. I don't know whether to feel cross at the extravagance—you could probably buy a year's worth of bacon for the same price at the supermarket—or simply greedy.

Anyway, it's been all action at work. Remember that man who bought the set for his fiancée? Today he was back. "Were larger panties necessary after all?" suggested Mother. Well, no. Not as such. In fact, no panties were necessary at all. Engagement was off. "Was it anything to do with the thong?" asked Mother. He shook his head as if it was the least of his worries.

"These foolish thongs," he said. Then he reddened, shuffled his feet, and asked if they did refunds. Sadly, Pritchard & Benning, Corsetières by Appointment to the Queen, does not offer refunds. No matter how tragic the circumstances. But he could have a credit. He stared at this dolefully and then turned to leave the shop. At the door he spun around, dashed back, and thrust it into her hands. "You have it," he said. "Do something with it.

You've been so kind. So understanding." And then he was gone.

That explains the pancetta and the good spirits.

🙜

In bed, later

Bert dropped by just as we were sitting down for supper. It's funny how he always seems to arrive at mealtimes. Mother gave him half of her spaghetti carbonara. I gave her a look and she said, "I'll fill up on bread." She told him the story of the man and the lingerie set right from the beginning. But all he said was, "Seventy quid? Is that how much that stuff costs? Just for a bit of French lace."

I'm sure he didn't mean to be rude. He's Julie's uncle and she loves him.

Then Mother took Marie and Cyril up to bed and Uncle Bert and I watched the news. It was all about the buildup to war, lots of soldiers marching and missiles being counted. They showed you a picture of a village that was near the firing line, some little children playing in the street with no shoes on. It made me think about the effect it would have on ordinary people. There was an expert talking about other ways of bringing about change, of different sorts of governmental policy, of stopping trade links and stuff like that. It seemed to make sense to me. I can't wait to talk about it with John The Pharmacist. But Uncle Bert started huffing and talking about small businesses and "who does he think he is, stupid bleeding-heart liberal."

I said I'd probably go on the school march and he got quite cross. He said, "What do you think a demonstration like that will achieve? It's just troublemaking. How many of you lot are old enough to have a properly thought-through opinion? Don't you realize the value of a show of might?"

I felt my face get hot. I told him I thought it was a mistake to assume all young people were politically apathetic.

He said, "Have you spared one thought for business?"

I've made up my mind. I'm definitely going on the march now.

Chapter Ten

Would you call me an activist? Maybe not, but I have done it. I've marched. I've marched, I've carried a banner, and now I'm home. The only problem is my head isn't full of an unjust war in a far-off place. It's full of my spat—could you call it a spat? Not really: more of a *situation*—with Julie.

It's been quite an afternoon. Fun and misery all mixed up. The whole school was there, or so it felt. We went all the way from school, down Hillcroft Road and the high street, to the river. "What do we want? Peace now. What do we want? Peace now." I've got it stuck in my brain.

I wanted to walk with Julie, but I looked for her everywhere and couldn't find her, so I went with William instead. He was on his bike—the idiot; it kept getting in the way. And we met Delilah, with her friend Sam, at the real estate agent's as planned. Delilah and Sam were all giggly. I had to have words with D about her outfit. "Delilah," I said, "do you really think combats are the thing?"

She looked horrified. "Are they finished?" she said. "Is no one at your school wearing them?"

I said, "Delilah, it's just it's a peace march, that's all."

She was carrying a big plastic bag and she dropped it. "I hate myself," she said. "I get everything wrong." Poor Delilah. She tends to do that—lurch from one mood to the next. William told her no one would notice, that he loved her Puma sneakers, and added, "Anyway, at least you're not wearing tweeds and wellies like Miss I'm-Too-Square-to-Get-a-Boyfriend here." I'd have knocked him off his bike if we hadn't been passing the drugstore. John was at the window and he gave a big thumbs-up and a peace sign when he saw us. It gave me a flutter of pleasure.

At the river things were a bit less organized. I think we were supposed to be crossing the bridge, but they had police there to stop us. The river was low and kids were assembling at the bottom of the slipway. There was some serious chanting, but a few boys were mucking about with a shopping cart, giving each other rides, and others were trying to climb up to the bridge from the bank. I kept looking around for Julie, but I couldn't see her. William said he was going then—we were really near the pub where his dad drinks and he probably didn't want to bump into him—so I turned around to ask Delilah if she wanted to walk home too and saw that she'd wandered off. She was at the bottom of the slipway, with her plastic bag open, handing out what looked like leaflets to everyone who passed. I clambered down to join her and only then, seeing the amusement on people's faces, saw what the leaflets were. *Invitations.* To a *party.*

"Delilah!" I said, lunging. "Put those invitations away."

I tried to grab the plastic bag from her, but she grabbed it back. I grabbed again and this time she let go and I felt myself do one of those comedy windmills as I tried to keep my balance. But the problem with wellies—where they fall down in relation to, say, Puma sneakers—is grip.

"Oh," said Delilah, looking down at me. She started laughing hysterically. The invitations had scattered all around me.

And, naturally, according to Sod's Law of personal relationships, that was when Julie came up.

"What *are* you doing?" she said. She was wearing her short white jacket with the belt.

Delilah, still laughing, said, "Picking up my invitations. Would you like one?"

Julie said drily, "I've already got one. I think most people have. Not a great idea giving them out to everyone unless you're prepared to accommodate the whole school. Are you?"

I was scrambling to my feet. I know Julie and Delilah don't get on, but it was as if Julie was being particularly mean to Delilah to get at me. It was horrible. I said lamely, "That's what I was trying to tell you, Delilah."

"Yeah, all right," she said, suddenly hoity-toity, and walked off.

So that was another friend I'd alienated. Then I asked Julie if she was off and she said yes, and I said did she want me to walk her to the bus stop and she said all right. But she didn't talk to me at all on the way, and when we got there a bus was just pulling in and she ran for it. As it moved off, I waved and scrunched my face up to make it try and say "What's wrong and why aren't you talking to me?" She didn't entirely ignore me. She gave a sort of half smile like she wanted to do more, but something was stopping her.

It seems self-obsessed and frivolous that I should end the day flustered about a spat with my best friend. But I can't help it. Half of me wants to call her up and plead with her to like me again. The other half is furious with her for making me feel like this. Why should I call her when I've done nothing wrong?

We should be beyond things like this. We're not children. We're fourteen, for goodness sake.

Chapter Eleven

FRIDAY, FEBRUARY 28
School library, 1:20 p.m.

I've had lunch but was too miserable to eat a thing. I've decided to lurk in the school library during break to lick my wounds. I just saw Julie outside the gym, giggling with Carmen. She stopped and looked away when I passed. I stuck out my tongue behind their backs. Proud? *Moi?*

I could go and find William or someone, but sometimes there is comfort in the company of other nerds— "the Library Crew" as Julie calls us when she needs help with her essays. I'm sitting next to Stacey Evans—or I was until she went to the loo. She's quite nice. Bit dull, but not the sort of person to go off you for no reason. She's very excited about the French exchange. "I'm surprised you're not going. Don't you have French blood, Connie?" she said. "Or isn't it your cup of tea?"

"Not my *tasse de thé*," I said gloomily. An airmail

letter with a French stamp arrived for Mother this morning. I saw her put it straight in the bin. I wonder when I get home whether I might not take it out and answer it myself. I wonder what my grandparents would think if they heard from me. I might give them both a heart attack with the shock.

Mr. Patrick, our class teacher, has just come in to put away some books. He's wearing thick beige corduroy trousers that make his legs look very stumpy. I'm rather painfully alert to the physical appearance of any male I come across at the moment. I spent geography comparing the muscle tone in the shoulders of the boys in front of me. I had to share a book with Joseph Milton and became fixated on the texture of his skin. Worst of all, in French oral I couldn't tear my eyes away from Mr. Baker's nipples, which you could just about see through his thin white shirt. I mustn't confess that to anyone. *Ever*. (He's been very sweet to me about not going on the French exchange, so I mustn't be too mean.)

As for Uncle Bert, there's just *too much* of him for my liking. His hair is too long and flouncy, his buttons are too undone, and his jeans are too tight. He wears a copper bracelet on one wrist, which he says is for arthritis. I must say I find it odd that a man so concerned with seeming young should so openly advertise the creakiness of his bones.

Oh, hang on. Here's Stacey back from the loo. Looking agitated.

Oh no. Bell's about to go. Here's what Stacey saw.

She rushed up to me and dragged me to the girls' toilets. In the second cubicle to the left, on the inside of the door, someone had written, "Delilah is a slut."

Now Stacey knows Delilah. She used to be in Brownies with her or something. She, like me, thinks there is probably only one set of parents in southeast England mean enough to call their daughter Delilah; that there is definitely only one set of parents mean enough to do so within graffiti distance of Woodvale Secondary's first-floor girls' loo.

We stared at her name in silence. Stacey said, "What are you going to do? You're going to have to do something."

"Like rub it off?" I said.

"No, like talk to her. She's getting A Reputation. Ask Julie. She'll tell you."

So, shall I? Shall I ask Julie?

The bell's gone. More later.

I'm home now. Amid internal and external turmoil. Mr. Spence has started work on the kitchen roof. He's in there now, with his ladder and his tools, causing havoc. He's taken some of the tiles off and put some polystyrene sheet up instead. It's not a peaceful thing, but alive and vicious; it's rattling and lunging in the wind and making me more edgy than I already am. As is the holey nature of the paint-splattered tracksuit bottoms he's wearing. He's so creepy. "Hello, hello, hello," he said when I came in. "What do we have here, then?"

"A fourteen-year-old girl who happens to live in this house," I said snippily before taking up residence on the sofa, which is where I am now. It's cold and grubby. Mother's clothes from yesterday are hanging over the armchair. The fridge has been moved in here to make room, and it's lurking next to the TV like some kind of big greasy white monster. The Delilah graffiti is lurking in my head like something equally big and greasy. There's only one thing for it. I'm going to swallow my pride and ring Julie.

❧

Oh. Oh. Oh.

I *wish* I hadn't done that.

Our conversation:

Me: "Hi. It's me."

Julie: "Oh, hello."

Me: "How are you?"

Julie: "Fine, thanks."

"I haven't really had a chance to talk to you since Sunday."

"I've been a bit, you know, busy."

"Nothing's wrong, is there?"

"No. Why should there be?"

"I just . . . Oh, never mind. Look, why I'm ringing is something awful's happened. Someone's written 'Delilah is a slut' in the first-floor girls' loos."

"Yeah. I know."

"But isn't it awful?"

"Yeah—" Little laugh. "Well, she shouldn't have got off with Darius, Toyah Benton's boyfriend, should she?"

"Toyah Benton?" Toyah Benton is a large, loud Shazzer who wears shiny red tracksuits and gold-hoop earrings. You wouldn't want to mess with Toyah Benton. "Her boyfriend? *When?*"

"Down at the river."

"What? After the march? How d'you know?"

"Carmen saw them. As did several others. Toyah Benton's well out to get her."

"But—"

"I've really got to go."

"Julie—"

"What?"

"What shall I do?"

"You could tell her to leave Darius alone."

"What about Toyah being out to get her? Should I warn her?"

"I don't know. She's your friend."

Oh. I *wish* I hadn't rung. She was so icy. Normally she throws herself headlong into any moral or social dilemma. And she was so hard on Delilah, like she thought she *was* a slut. And she isn't, is she? I've always thought of Delilah as being v innocent, as experimenting, or collecting. It's as if she's discovered something that she quite likes and she keeps having more of it—like ice cream or chocolate fingers—and no one's telling her to stop. She's not hurting anybody. (Quite the opposite.) And it's not like she goes the whole way or anything. I don't think.

Oh no, here she is. . . . I'm going to nab her.

I'm back. Mission accomplished. *Not.*

"Hey, Delilah," I said, shooting out of our front door. "What gives?"

She said, "Nothing," rather defensively. I might have looked a bit suspicious.

"Can I come around?"

"Yeah. Okay."

We went into the house, greeted her mother, and headed up to her room. She kicked off her shoes, climbed the ladder, and threw herself on to her bed.

"God, life's boring," she said. "I wish something would happen." There was a sort of desperate, yearning expression on her face.

I climbed the ladder up on to the platform and sat cross-legged at her feet, fiddling with Floppy Elephant. I wasn't quite sure how to broach the subject. Should I warn her directly about Toyah or give her a bit of general moral guidance? I decided, considering her mood, on the latter.

"Delilah," I began, "this weekend—"

"I might go down to the youth club later," she interrupted. "Do you know if William's going?"

I said I didn't.

"Tomorrow I might go bowling with Sam, or some of the girls in my class are meeting at that new shopping center down the A3. Or I might go to the cinema, and I've got to tidy up my room and—" She broke off and gave a strangulated moan.

"What's the matter?" I said, wondering if she already *knew*.

"This weekend, it's just . . . Oh God. This boy I like's having a party."

"A boy? You mean Darius?"

"No." She looked at me as if I was mad. "Who? You mean that bloke at the river? No, of course not. No, he's called Dan Curtis. He's one of the boys I got off with on Saturday. He's having a party this weekend and he hasn't even invited me." It turns out someone called Sally at her school who *hadn't* got off with him *was* invited and had been making her life a misery all week for the fact that she wasn't.

I got a bit confused about who was and who wasn't and who had and who hadn't. Sometimes it's as if the whole world goes to parties that I don't go to. But it was a good moment for the moral bit, so I said, "Del. Maybe *getting off* with someone immediately like that isn't the best way of *getting on*."

She looked at me witheringly, if you can look witheringly through eyes as big and blue and tear-filled as hers, and said, "Oh yeah? What are you saying?"

I said, "Maybe you should wait until you really like someone before letting them kiss you." I trailed away. "You know, as in Darius down at the river . . ."

She didn't seem to hear this last bit. "I don't let *them* kiss *me. I* kiss *them."

"That's what I mean. But maybe you should wait for someone really nice. You know, find out if they are The One first."

She looked scandalized. "Oh, right. And just hang around, like some uptight weirdo, waiting for nothing, like you? No thanks."

I managed to say, "Fair enough. Maybe steer clear of other people's boyfriends, then, that's all."

She swung her legs over the bed and looked at me intently. "Who are we talking about? William?"

"No." I laughed, shaking my head as if it had bugs in it. "Of course not. Just be careful, that's all."

&

8 p.m.

That was a few hours ago. Since then William's been around, hanging about Mother's ankles, looking hungry. She fussed over him, getting all French and "ooh la la," making toast and telling him she could see his hipbones.

Yeah, right. Whose fault is that for wearing jeans two sizes too big?

Mr. Spence finished work for the day and didn't leave. Maybe he wanted toast or "ooh la la"ing too. And then Jack turned up with his new girlfriend, Dawn, who's tall and skinny. Usually Jack throws Cyril and Marie around the place, and makes them shriek with laughter, but when he's got a new girlfriend with him he gets all awkward and cool as if he doesn't know whether to show his new girlfriend what a great dad he is, or stand back, cool and narrow-eyed, reminding Mother what a great catch he is. He met Dawn selling fish door-to-door. She bought a box of Dublin Bay prawns and a duo of stuffed plaice. Must be love. Never is, though.

"This," Jack said, lunging, when I came into the room, "is my favorite stepdaughter in the world."

I reared back. Lately, this house is either Odor of Calvin or Odor of Cod. "I'm your *only* stepdaughter in the world," I said. "Don't show off."

Jack turned to New Dawn and said, "See what I have to put up with?"

There was tooting outside the house in the street then. Mother, still chatting to Mr. Spence, shrieked at me that it was Bert and she wasn't ready and could I run and tell him to come in?

This I did. He humphed at me through the car window but went and parked. He came in and stood around, one hand inside his shirt, massaging his own shoulder. He said "Ciao" to everyone in a fake-friendly sort of way. William gave me A Look (I know why—we hate it when grown-ups are overly chummy, and we hate "ciao"). Mr. Spence, coming late into the room, said, "Evening all," to which nobody answered. Then Mother went upstairs and Uncle Bert got all snippy with Marie. She'd been making a camp next to the fridge in the sitting room—using all the cushions from the sofa—and when Uncle B. realized there was nowhere to sit, I heard him say, "Hey. You. Scram." Marie looked too shocked to scream.

Then everyone left—William went home to leave lettuce out for his hamster, Mother and Uncle B. went out, and J, D, M, and C went to McDonald's. I declined the offer of this last and mooched around downstairs on my own. I searched the trash for the airmail letter Mother got this morning, but I couldn't find it.

I'm too depressed to breathe, let alone eat. It's been such a miserable day. One of my best friends is a slut; the other isn't talking to me.

And is Delilah right? Am I an uptight weirdo? Am I waiting around for nothing? Recently I've had this yearning, restless feeling inside me. I don't want a boyfriend. I don't want love. I definitely don't want anyone's hands up my sweater. (It's not that I'm too young, it's just, having been through it all with Mother, I'm too *grown-up* for all that.) I don't know what's wrong. I've just got this funny aching feeling that something—everything—more interesting is going on elsewhere.

&

In bed, 2 a.m.

And don't get me started on Uncle Bert.

> 1. *Money: if he's so rich, how comes he never pays for anything? And happily eats us out of house and home?*

> 2. *French leanings: he thinks French wine is overpriced. That lingerie "French lace" comment. And all this stuff about French lessons. Isn't it just a way to get a free meal?*

> 3. *Small children: beeping from the car (avoidance); his irritation with Marie; his attitude to Woodvale's march; his use of the word "scram."*

I've had enough of this notebook.

Chapter Twelve

The drugstore, quiet moment, 4:30 p.m.

I faced up to the truth during the long, dark night. Everything has gone wrong. And it's all my fault. I've meddled. I've created my own Frankenstein's monster.

I never thought I'd write in here again. This beautiful, deliciously smelling notebook would be wasted forever. But today everything has changed.

The morning began dull and overcast. You couldn't believe spring would ever come. The drugstore was dark when I arrived. John was in the back eating a bacon sandwich and reading the newspaper. He only has a microwave at home, he told me, and crispy bacon's apparently one thing you miss when you only have a microwave at home. He gets his bacon sandwiches from the cafe at the station. Sometimes he has one for lunch, too.

"You all right?" he said. But he obviously didn't know anything was up because he didn't leave enough space for me to answer before saying, "Start on the shampoos, would you?"

The boxes were just by his feet, so I crouched down next to him with the price gun. He was wearing his jeans and a pair of worn brown shoes that he had only half shoved on over bare feet so his heels were squashing down the leather at the back. I started with the Neutrogenas. When I got to the anti-dandruff ones I wondered whether to say anything (you know, like, "My mother's favorite, this"), but the click of the price gun seemed loud in the silence and I felt too self-conscious.

After a bit he folded up his newspaper. "Ah, Connie," he said. "You're making me feel guilty. Time to open up."

He spun the sign and beep-beeped the register. Then he came back into the pharmacy section and put his white coat on over his jeans. He's so dark—dark bristly hair, dark knitted eyebrows, dark deep-set eyes—the white coat makes him look like a rook pretending to be a seagull. A few people came in and I went through to serve them. Gail was going to be late because her mother was in the hospital with her hip. John seemed distracted. He sorted out some antibiotics for someone, but didn't say much. I never know how much he notices me. I wonder if I was older—I mean really older, like twenty or something—he'd be aware of the silences and feel socially obliged to fill them. It must be something to do with the professional nature of our relationship, but oddly for me I don't feel I can ask questions or volunteer information unless *encouraged.*

So it was a relief when a bit later he said, "You're looking very solemn today."

I told him I was just tired.

"Hard night?"

I suspect he meant out at the pub like any normal sixteen-year-old, not lying awake worrying about the disastrous marriage she may have arranged for her only parent.

I said I was fine. After a bit I said, "By the way, do you remember what you said about not having met any-body who supported the war?"

"Yes."

"Well, I have now."

"Oh?"

"Yep. My mother's boyfriend says the buildup has had a knock-on effect on business or something, that you can't beat a show of might. He says demonstrations are 'troublemaking.'"

"Takes all sorts."

I've noticed when people say "takes all sorts," a phrase that supposedly celebrates the different opinions that make up the world, they're actually being critical. I felt an internal shiver of satisfaction, but also dread, when he said this. It was lovely to hear someone say something against Bert—and it's made me see, if he's pro-war, he can't be nice, can he? But it was also scary to have my feelings confirmed. I'm in so deep. What if I can't undo what we've done?

More customers came in. And while I was working through the line, Gail arrived, looking flustered and matronly at the same time.

"You're looking a bit peaky, Connie," she said once she'd talked a young mother through the prepared baby-food range. "Are you working too hard at school? When are your finals again?" She peeled off the lid of the cup of takeout coffee she'd bought with her and took a sip. Her face cleared. "Hm. Heaven," she said. "I love a mocha."

I feel easier when she's in the shop, which is funny because John is so nice and *doesn't ask about finals*. It's just having more people around, I suppose. I told her I was working quite hard at school, exams not for a bit (NB for confessional purposes: that's evasion, not deceit), but that I was a bit miserable because I'd fallen out with a friend. I'm so glad I did. John was sorting other people's photographs into envelopes—he's quite strict about us not seeing for privacy reasons—and had his back to us.

Her face contracted. "Oh no. Have you? Oh. What was that over, then?" I couldn't answer because we had a rash of parents and children to deal with, small hands reaching for the diabetic chocolate; long debate over Calpol with sugar versus Calpol without. John sidled into the back when this was going on. He's not great with mothers, and Gail tends to give either too much advice or not enough. As usual I found myself talking about my little brother and sister; personal recommendations seem to be what customers like. Anyway, they all trooped out at last.

I said, "I think I offended her."

"Who, dear?"

"My friend. I've upset her somehow."

"Her? Not a *boy*friend, then?"

"No!"

"So what happened? What did you do to offend her?"

"I don't know."

"Well, you should ask her and then you will know."

I felt a fat tear welling out of my eye. Sympathy is always a killer.

She had time to say, "Oh dear," before dealing with another customer. Back at the register, she whispered, "Why don't you give her a call? Sort it out. I'm sure it's nothing."

I blew my nose and nodded.

I didn't do it immediately. I waited until John went to

the bank at lunchtime. Then I went to the phone at the back. I felt nervous, but Gail was looking at me and nodding encouragement.

She wasn't at her mom's. So I tried her at her dad's. Alison answered. She said, "Oh, hello, Carmen. I'll just get her," and I almost hung up. I only managed to fit in, "It's Connie," before she was yelling up the stairs.

Julie took a few minutes to come. "Hello," she said, without expression.

"Julie. It's Connie," I said unnecessarily.

She said, "Hello," again, this time with artificial brightness.

I said, "Why are you being funny with me?"

"I'm not being funny with you."

I said, "Why aren't you talking to me, then?"

Still in the same false tone, she said, "I am talking to you. I'm talking to you now."

"Yes, but not properly."

"Yes, I am," she said. Long silence.

"See?" I said.

Gail was making further gestures with her hands. Eventually I asked if Julie would meet me and she said, "When?"

I said, "Sometime today?"

She said, "Maybe I'll drop in if I'm passing."

And then we both hung up and that was that. I stayed

out the back for a bit, staring at the boxes of shampoos. Friendship is so hard and painful. I can't imagine ever being able to deal with love.

But then John got back from the bank and Gail was busy at the register, so I carried on with my shampoos. I think Gail might have told him I was down, because he went out again and bought us a sandwich platter to share from Marks & Spencer. We ate them in a huddle. I wouldn't eat the shrimp or the tuna ones because of fish overload. "Sorry to look a sea horse in the mouth," I said, and explained about Jack. John seemed to find it very funny. I even told him about the Newcastle accent Jack sometimes puts on when he goes door-to-door, which I haven't told anyone. John laughed as if I'd really tickled him and I felt a warm glow inside.

Julie came at three o'clock. Later I discovered she wasn't passing at all. She was supposed to be going to the cinema with Carmen and she'd canceled. Sometimes one can get people so wrong.

She stood by the nail varnishes with a funny expression on her face. John said I could nip out for half an hour if I liked. Gail said, "Go on."

Julie and I walked in silence to the cafe by the station and sat at a table in the window. I ordered a Coke; she ordered a Diet Coke. It was hot in there. My can was warm; her can, from farther back in the fridge, had pearls of condensation on the outside. I should have got a Diet one too. But I hate aspartame. I hate all artificial sweetness.

"Thanks for coming," I said.

She said, "I was passing anyway."

I told her I liked her new top. It was pale blue and cap-sleeved and had a picture of a girl surfing a large wave on it. She looked down at it, as if noticing it for the first time, and said, "Oh."

"So here we are," I said.

"Here we are," she replied woodenly.

Irritation spurred me on. "Oh, come on, Julie. What have I done? Please tell me. This is ridiculous."

She pretended for a while, all hoity-toity, that I hadn't done anything, that it was all fine, but I kept on and finally—finally—in a rush, she said, "Okay. I was really offended when you didn't walk down the hill with me."

"When?"

"On Tuesday. On the march."

I was confused because this wasn't like her and also it didn't seem to tally with the timing—wasn't she already funny on the phone on Sunday?—but I didn't want to lose the moment, so I said, "I'm really sorry. It was obviously a misunderstanding. I did look for you, but I thought you'd gone ahead."

She gave a small smile.

"Can we be friends now, then?" I said.

She nodded. "Yeah. Okay. So how've you been?"

We chatted, but we didn't look at each other. Or we did, but in an odd way. If I was talking—telling her about Mr. Spence and the flat roof—I looked at her, but she kept her eyes on the table. And when she was talking—telling me about the kind of dye she'd used for her hair last weekend—I found my eyes going elsewhere. (I did an experiment on this at home later. When people are relaxed, it's the other way around; the person who's *talking* looks around, but the person who's *listening* keeps their eyes on them.) We'd finished our Cokes and had begun walking back to the drugstore when tentatively I mentioned the graffiti about Delilah. She laughed knowingly, "Oh yeah."

I said, "Do you think Toyah Benton really is 'out to get her'?"

She said, "I don't know. The problem is, she knows where Delilah lives."

"How?"

"How do you think?"

"I don't know."

"She's got an invitation to her party."

I stopped in my tracks to take in a sharp breath. Julie looked at me and raised her eyebrows. We stared at each other and then we both burst out laughing.

By the time we reached the door to the drugstore, and had discussed Delilah's behavior in minute detail (how far exactly had she gone with Toyah Benton's boyfriend? Would Toyah come to Delilah's party to seek revenge?), things seemed to be back to normal.

"See you on Monday," I said. "And I'm sorry about the march. I guess I just got . . . swept up in the moment."

"Bye," she answered. I made as if to go in, but as she didn't move, I turned again.

"Bye," I said.

She was still standing there. "Connie?"

I had my hand on the door. "Yes?"

"Look, about the march—"

"Yes?"

She sighed. "I've been a cow."

I had to step back out of the doorway on to the sidewalk to make room for a middle-aged woman exiting in a hurry.

Julie was frowning and twisting her thumb in the top buttonhole of her denim jacket. "I lied. I wasn't cross with you about that."

"Weren't you?"

"No. I wasn't really cross with you about anything. It was nothing you did. It's just . . ."

"It's just what?"

She looked down at the pavement. "Nothing."

"No. Tell me."

She pulled me to one side, into the doorway that leads to the flat above the pharmacist's. "It's Uncle Bert."

"Uncle Bert?"

"I think we made a mistake—"

"Do you?" I felt the flickerings of hope. "Why?"

"It's just . . . Do you think they're right for each other?"

"I don't know. Maybe not." I was still being careful.

"It's just . . . I know we engineered it. That we did it. But it was just a game. Wasn't it? I never thought it would work." Her eyes darted this way and that. She lowered her voice to a whisper. "I mean, did you? It was just a game. And now he's around your house all the time, and taking you lot out for Chinese and . . . It's just, he's my uncle. . . ."

It was taking a while for it to sink in. I said, "Is this because you don't think they're right for each other, or because you don't really want him seeing Mother?"

She twisted her lip with her teeth. "Um . . ."

"It's all right," I said. "You can tell the truth. I don't mind."

She looked at me, directly in the eyes. "If they're in love with each other and everything, then that's fine, but if they're not . . . It's just he's not bored anymore, he doesn't drop in at our house all the time, and he doesn't feel like he belongs to me anymore." She shook her head. "But that's fine, if they're happy. I'm not a little girl. I'm too old to be jealous. I'll just have to come and see him at your house. . . ."

All sorts of things were racing through my mind: happiness that we were friends, but also relief about something else. It was like being at the bottom of the water and seeing light glimmering on the surface and realizing it only needed a few pushes to get there. I said, "He's not around our house all the time."

"Isn't he?"

"No. He honks from the street."

Julie, who had been looking like she might be about to cry (which is very unlike her), gave a little laugh. "Does he leave the engine running?" she asked.

"And the door open," I said.

We smiled at each other. I put my hand on her shoulder and told her that I understood everything and that we should meet to talk about it more. I said, "I just wish you'd told me, that's all. Not ignored me."

She said, "Sorry," in a very small voice, and gave me a hug.

I kept my own anxieties concerning Uncle Bert's status as stepfather material to myself. There was no point upsetting her. I suggested she came around this evening to talk about the next step—splitting them up.

She grimaced. "Can't. Not tonight. Sorry. Going to Dan Curtis's sixteenth."

"Who is Dan Curtis?" I said. "Why does everyone else know him and I don't?"

"You never go out, that's why," she said, but there was affection in her voice.

She's coming around tomorrow instead.

Julie and I have done a terrible, dangerous thing.

But what we have done, we can undo.

Chapter Thirteen

SUNDAY, MARCH 2
The bathroom, 4 p.m.

I'd almost given up on Julie when she finally turned up today. We'd been to Mass and I'd helped Cyril find "Five Interesting Facts About the Tudors" for his homework. Then Marie had remembered she needed to be a Victorian child for tomorrow's assembly and Mother went into a spin trying to find something. I suggested a shower cap and an apron, and a new attitude. Seen but not heard and all that. Marie just wanted to wear pink and had a fit. Honestly, for a little angel she can be quite demonic.

Over lunch (sandwiches because of the roofless nature of the kitchen), Mother told us she was going out again tonight—she was giving Bert "another lesson." I panicked for a moment, but calmed myself with the thought that Julie would be here soon, that together we would think of something. I was putting Marie's hair into a bun when the doorbell went.

It was Julie. She was wearing jeans, a baggy sweatshirt, and what looked like last night's makeup (smeary): a dressed-down Sunday look. She glanced at Mother, who was hanging out some underwear on the drying rack. "Hiya, Bernadette."

Mother looked up and waved. She was dangling some sort of damp purple lace thing from her fingers. Julie and I looked at each other—too much information—and went upstairs.

In my bedroom Julie threw herself on to the bed and closed her eyes.

"How was Dan Curtis's party?" I said.

She groaned. "I need sleep. More sleep."

"Late night?"

She opened one of her eyes and gave me a dark look. "Could say that."

"Was it good?"

She groaned again. She was behaving like she was really relaxed, but I knew it was partly an act.

I said, "I'm so glad you came. I'm so glad we're friends again," and smiled at her.

She sat up and stretched. When she'd finished, her shoulders sort of crumpled in on themselves in a hunch. She looked at me sheepishly. "Me too," she said. "Ow."

She shifted her bottom, so she could take something from the back pocket of her jeans. Her phone. She studied it and laid it on my bedside table, facing her. For the next ten minutes she kept checking the display. "Delilah was there," she said airily. "Making a right fool of herself."

"Not again," I said, then remembered. "But I thought she wasn't invited."

"Yeah, well, however she got in, she got into the spirit of things when she did."

"What do you mean?" I sat next to Julie on the bed as dread began to curl its way down my legs.

Julie's eyes were laughing. When she spoke it was with something that sounded like admiration. She mouthed the words more than spoke them. "Took her top off."

"What?"

"I think she'd had loads to drink. And she was getting into dancing, really saucily. She had some boys from St. Antony's around her. And next time I looked over she had taken her top off and was spinning it above her head. Everyone was whooping and . . . well, you know, it was a private-school crowd. Some of the boys thought they'd died and gone to heaven. There were just a few of us in the corner looking a bit dubious."

"Oh. My. God." What had happened to the Delilah I used to play doll's houses with, the Delilah who owned

Floppy Elephant? "Was Toyah Benton there?"

"Different crowd."

I wanted to ask more about it, but Julie was getting out a notebook from the inside pocket of her parka.

"To business," she said. "I'm so glad I'm right about your mom and Uncle Bert and that you agree with me. But we're going to have to work fast. They've been seeing each other for two weeks and"—she leaned forward to check her phone—"any minute now, we're talking LTR."

"LTR?"

"Long-Term Relationship. Much harder to destroy. You've got habit as well as affection to deal with then. Now. I've had a few thoughts. It's clear to me that part of Uncle Bert's attraction to your mom is her availability. . . ."

"Steady on," I said.

"No. I don't mean that rudely. I just mean Sue had gone off to Australia and there was your mom, pretty and flattered and in need of saving. I know my uncle. He was bored. He was hungry. He always needs a woman to feed him. If it had been a bit hard, on the other hand, he wouldn't have bothered. What was that Shakespeare thing we did in English last year? 'Thou shalt not to true love admit impediments'? Something like that. Anyway, impediments are not Uncle Bert's thing. So. We need to make it hard for him."

"How would we do that?" A memory of Marie's last

tantrum came into my mind.

"That's what we need to discuss."

"We'd better be quick," I said. "They're out again tonight."

"Okay." She checked the display on her phone again. Then lay forward on the bed, on her stomach, with a pen in her hand and the notebook resting on the pillow. I paced the room, occasionally pausing to stare out of the window up at the sky, or down at the patchwork quilt of suburban gardens, stitched with fences. Finally we came up with a list that went like this:

IMPEDIMENTS
1. Make it hard for Bernadette to see Uncle Bert.
Cancel babysitter (do this tonight?). Fake illness.
Pass on false messages. Generally bugger it up.

2. Put Bernadette off Bert, and Bert off
Bernadette. Besmirch characters, spread
malicious rumors. Hide Bernadette's makeup.

3. Find new love interest for Bernadette.

Most of this came from Julie. Point three was my addition. I insisted. After all, it was Operation New Man that began all this.

Every few minutes while we were plotting, Julie would check on her phone. We were about to refer to our initial list when it finally rang. Well, I say rang. It actually played the chorus from the Electric B'stards' number-one single, "Spit on My Shoes."

Julie leaped up, grabbed the phone, and then sat on the edge of the bed holding it in her palm for a few bars before answering. When she did, she said, "Hell-o," on a half laugh as if she was in the middle of sharing a joke with someone. "Oh. Hi." She sounded cool, slightly surprised to have heard from whoever it was. "This afternoon? Oh. Um. Let me think." She put her hand over the phone, waited, and then lifted it. She was so offhand I was sure she was going to say no. "Er, actually that should be okay. The UGC at five-thirty? Sure. See you." When she hung up, she clasped the phone to her breast and closed her eyes. "Connie," she said, "I am in love."

"Oh yes?"

She opened them. "He's called Ade. He was at Dan Curtis's party."

"And?"

"He's gorgeous. He's at St. Antony's—doing his senior year. Quite sophisticated, but well fit."

Apparently she and Carmen had been outside the party, which was in the recreation center, having a ciggie on the swings, and he'd come up and bummed a light.

They'd ended up messing around outside for a while. He'd climbed up the frame of the swing and hung upside down from the bar and then Carmen had got cold and had gone back into the party, and Julie and Ade had talked for ages and then he'd walked her home. They'd spent her cab money on chips and had sat on the wall outside her house sharing them and talking some more until her mom had banged on the bathroom window and Julie had to go in.

Partly I loved hearing about this. She was so funny doing an imitation of her mom's face, peering out into the darkness without her specs on, but a tiny bit of me felt envious and yearning. I sort of wished I'd gone to the party. I mean, even Cinder-delilah had in the end. Would I have felt out of place, like I always think I will?

"And now he's asked you on a date," I said. I was doing pretend sixties dancing with my arms, rolling them around with one flying out, to illustrate excitement, and to hide the fact I was feeling left out. I was wearing my zip-up mohair cardigan and a pair of baggy men's trousers. "And you're seeing him—when?"

Julie looked at her watch and rubbed her forehead. "Oh God. In a couple of hours. I'd better go home and put on my war paint."

I was still doing my silly jerky dance. "You. Better. Had."

She went ahead of me down the stairs. "So, Mission Breakup. Are you on the case? You've got to think of a way to stop Jack from babysitting tonight."

I followed, jogging down each step one by one. "Yup," I said. I don't know why I was behaving so stupidly. I expect I was still feeling a little self-conscious around her and also a bit disappointed that, after everything, she was leaving so soon.

But Julie turned when she reached the bottom of the first flight and watched me. She was laughing. "Con," she said, "in all seriousness, do you think it might be time you bought a wired bra?"

That was two hours ago. Since then, I have studied myself in the mirror, stationary and joggling, sideways and front on. Julie is right. There is quite a lot of movement there now. But do I really have to get a proper upholstered bra? I don't want one. Is it because I don't want to grow up? It can't be that. I *am* grown-up. When I was, like, five, people were telling me how grown-up I was. I like my undershirts. They're cozy and safe. Real bras look so uncomfortable. I can see the purple lacy one Mother was hand washing earlier on the line. I'm going to experiment.

I've just sneaked down and slipped it off the dryer to bring it back up to the bathroom. Cyril saw me. "What are you doing with Mother's bra?" he said. I just glared at him and ran past. It's still a bit damp, but the main problem is it was actually too small. I'd need a bigger one. Oh Lord.

&

My room, 9 p.m.

I had to have a lie down to recover from the bra exertions, and was reclining on the sofa when the doorbell went. Mother opened the door. It was William.

"You all right?" he said, squatting down next to me on the floor. He was wearing baggy army shorts, a washed-out red T-shirt with a torn neck and writing you couldn't read, and his huge, new, gleaming white sneakers. I noticed the muscles on his calves, and the pale inner thighs where there aren't any hairs.

"Where've you been?" I asked him.

"Playing tennis with my brother."

"Glad you've made some concession to whites," I said, nodding at his Nikes.

"No one cares down at the rec," he said. "You ill?"

"Malingering," I said truthfully.

He stood up and put out his hands to pull me off the sofa. "Come on, let's go for a bike ride down the towpath. It's quite sunny out. Unless you've got homework."

"I've done it," I said. "Did it on Friday afternoon."

He grinned at me. "'Course you did."

∴ 114 ∾

It was sunny down by the river, warm on the back of your neck. William raced ahead of me. He's still wearing his pant elastic above his shorts. He turned back once. "Having a bit of trouble with your old men's trews?" he hollered, which made me put on an extra spurt to catch up with him. It's bumpy along the towpath, and you have to slow down for the occasional ambling family group, but we cycled alongside each other most of the way. I'd forgotten my lingerie crisis and was filled with good spirits, and relief. William has that effect on me sometimes. And I don't think I'd realized how unhappy the Uncle Bert thing had made me. I *knew* he was wrong for Mother, but couldn't face up to it with Julie behaving so oddly toward me in case it made things worse between us. Now both anxieties had been cleared up in one fell swoop. All I had to do was think of a way to prevent their date tonight. And it was sunny at last. So bugger bras.

When we reached the boathouse we threw our bikes on the ground and ran down the ramp to the sludgy beach below. "What are you smiling about?" William asked.

"Nothing." I picked up a pebble and skimmed it across the gray water. "I've made up with Julie."

William was trying to hit a buoy several meters into the river. "What was all that about, then?

"I don't know. But it's all right now."

"Funny girl."

"Who? Me or her?"

"Julie."

"She is not."

"She is. Likes things her own way."

"At least she's not spoiled like Delilah."

"Delilah's not spoiled, she's messed up." His last stone hit the buoy. "There's a difference."

"I know," I said. "Did you hear what she did last night?"

"Who? Julie?"

"No. Delilah."

"Did I *hear* about it? I *saw* it. Or *them*, I should say."

"Oh." The impact of William seeing Delilah topless was momentarily swept away by the realization that *everyone* I knew had been at Dan Curtis's the night before. "You were there too, then?"

"Yup. Poor little cow." He shrugged. "Anyway, I didn't see much. There were too many people around her. By the time I reached her, she had put her top back on. She was out of her head. I don't know how I got her home."

"You took her home? That was nice."

He looked a bit grim. "Someone had to."

"Julie was there too."

"I know. I saw her walking off with some bloke at the end."

We had sat down on the end of the ramp. The sun was getting low and I pulled my mohair cardigan around me and rested my chin on my knees. "He's called Ade. He's asked her out," I said, looking out at the river. I watched a couple of swans glide past a large piece of driftwood. "They've gone to the cinema."

One of the swans was floating away from the other, toward the bank, where the water gleamed like gasoline. William was saying something.

"Sorry?"

"I *said*, 'Do you fancy going to the cinema some-time?'"

"What?"

"The cinema."

"What about it?"

"Do you want to go sometime?"

The swan had drifted back toward its mate. It was feeling cooler now. I didn't have much time. How *was* I going to stop Mother going out with Bert tonight? Could I ring him and say Mother was ill? How could I do that without being found out? "Not really," I said absent-mindedly.

William cycled back with me to my house, but didn't come in. Delilah must have been watching from her window, though, because she was in his face before he had a chance to bike off. She was wearing her black Juicy track-suit, sparkly flip-flops, and big pink lipstick.

"Will, Will, Will," she said. "I made such an idiot of myself last night. I was just, like, wasted. How can I ever, ever thank you for being such an angel?"

"Hi, Delilah," I said.

"Sorry. Hello, Connie."

William—or should I call him "Will"?—muttered, "'S'all right."

I said, "I'm surprised you didn't get cold, that's all. I mean, it's only March."

She laughed and I felt mean.

William got on to his bike, muttering about home-work, and Delilah drifted back into her house. I went in, still trying to cook up a plan. My family was watching *101 Dalmatians*, for about the hundred and first time. Marie looked up when she saw me in the doorway and said, "Daddy's not coming because Mom's not going out, after all." I looked at Mother, who was in the armchair next to the fridge mending Cyril's school sweater. She said, "Bert rang. Something came up."

I stared at her, my mind racing. So I didn't need to think of a way to cancel Jack. Julie must have got to Uncle Bert first. What on earth could she have said to him? (I've just tried to call her, but she's still not back from the cinema.)

Then Cyril said, "I'm sad because I wanted to see Dad," which gave me a momentary pang. That's the problem with war. There are always innocent casualties.

After Cyril and Marie had gone to bed, Mother and I looked at the photo albums like we used to. There are pictures of her, a young girl in Paris, on the back of someone's Vespa. (*So* romantic.) There are pictures of a small smart couple, arms around each other, outside a church. Her parents. But she closed the book then and put it back. We watched the news—more soldiers, more politicians— and then we watched my father's video. She didn't look sad. In fact, even as I write I can hear her singing the jingle in the bathroom. "Cari, Cari, Carrrrib-vod." And if a tiny jolt of loneliness crossed her face when I said I was going up to bed, it has only hardened my resolve.

Chapter Fourteen

MONDAY, MARCH 3
My bedroom, 6 p.m.

Julie wasn't in school today, so I *still* don't know what she cooked up yesterday. V. frustrating. Carmen and I rang her from Carmen's mobile at break. We could hardly hear what she said, her throat was so bad. Tonsillitis, she thinks. She managed to whisper, "How's the project?" to me before her mother made her hang up.

Yikes. I thought I was off the hook. I suppose one canceled date does not a relationship break. I'd better get to it. Bad-mouthing, I think. Bad-mouthing I can manage.

Back from a trip downstairs, 7 p.m.

Mother was making tea for Mr. Spence, who was in the sitting room leaning against the shipwrecked fridge, wriggling his shoulders and rubbing his back in a "phew,

I've been busy with the old manual work today" sort of way. (I'm sure it's time he was getting home.)

I went to the bookshelf and said in a casual way, as if it was something that had been idly bothering me for a while, "How old would you say Bert is?"

Mother was holding the tea bag and dipping it in and out of the hot water. "I couldn't say," she said.

"Well, what do you think? Thirty-eight? Forty? I know he acts like a teenager, but he can't be much younger than Julie's mom and she's at least forty-five."

"Connie!" She gave me a steely look and then smiled at Mr. Spence as she handed him his mug. "I don't know. It's rude to comment like that."

Marie, bless her little cotton socks, piped up from the plate of spaghetti hoops she was eating at the table, "I think he's ugly."

"Marie!" Mother threw Mr. Spence another smile.

"And he smells."

Mother said, "Really!" and frowned, but I did a thumbs-up to Marie. Completely unrehearsed! Marie may well be an untapped resource.

Called Julie to tell her. Her mother says she's too ill to come to the phone.

Chapter Fifteen

TUESDAY, MARCH 4
Bedroom, 8 p.m.

*T*oday I started on Granny Enid.

She had just settled Marie and Cyril in front of the television and was standing in the kitchen doorway, giving Mr. Spence a pursed look. (She clearly doesn't think much of the way you can see his hairy legs through the holes in his tracksuit bottoms either.) Mother was late, so I had time to say, "Have you heard about this man Mother's giving French lessons to?"

She nodded. "Yes, isn't it good, dear?"

"No, it's not." I was whispering because of Mr. S. "He's not very nice."

"Constance!"

"He just isn't. He's . . ." I lowered my voice even further. "He's seeing other women."

Enid took a sharp intake of breath. I'd got her on a

raw spot. (She's never recovered from Jack's treatment of Mother.) "Poor lamb. Widowed at such an early age and then *shackled* to such a disaster of a man. . . ."

This distracted me. I always feel I need to stand up for Jack when even his mother's horrible about him. I said brightly, "The fish thing doesn't seem to be going too badly," but she just sniffed, as if she could smell it from there. I said, "Anyway, can you have a word with her about this bloke Bert?"

She shook her head. "I really don't think it's my place. Sssssh." Mr. Spence had materialized at my shoulder.

He said, "Sorry to disturb your little confabulation, but if it is all right with you two lovely ladies, I need to move, to redeploy, my ladder." Now he's more relaxed around our house—he should be, he bloody well lives in the place—he keeps putting on silly voices like this.

I raised my eyes to the ceiling and moved out of the way, and after that I didn't have a chance to say any more, because Granny E. realized the time and left, but at least I've planted a seed.

Chapter Sixteen

WEDNESDAY, MARCH 5
Sitting room, 5:30 p.m.

I 've progressed to wanton destruction. Desperate measures. I was late from school and came straight up to my room to avoid having to talk to Mr. Spence.

I ran down when I heard the phone ring, but he got there first. I heard him say, "Wandsworth Borough Lunatic Asylum. Only joking, how can I help? No, she's not here. I'll take a message, shall I?"

When I came down again later, Mother was home and Mr. S. had changed into his smart clothes. If you ask me, he definitely hangs around each night to see her.

"Bernadette," he said (no messing around with surnames anymore, I've noticed). "Could I have a little word about the . . . the roof tiles? In the garden. If that's all right?"

"John, of course," she said, and followed him out.

I watched them. He was talking, looking up at the roof. She was listening hard. At one point, she put her hand on his arm. I shuddered, looked away, and that was when I saw the piece of paper on the counter. It was a Sainsbury's receipt. And on the back of it Mr. Spence had written, "5:05 p.m.: Bert rang. He'll be in tonight. Please could you ring him back."

I inhaled sharply. So, he'd called. He hadn't been completely put off by Julie. *Yet.* I wavered for a moment and then I picked up the receipt, scrumpled it, and stuffed it into my pocket. Outside in the garden, I heard Mother say, "All I care about, John, is that it doesn't happen again." I paused, suddenly guilt struck. Her with a leaky kitchen roof and a flaky boyfriend. I took the receipt out of my pocket, smoothed it, and put it back on the table. But now it looked suspicious. Who would write a note on a crumpled receipt? It was too late. I picked it up, ran back up here, tore it into pieces, and ran down again.

They were coming in from the garden. Mother was laughing in a flirtatious way, stroking Marie's head at the same time. She was still wearing her coat and holding a bag from work. A shopping bag with Pritchard & Benning on the outside. Suddenly she turned and handed it to me. "I had to guess the size," she said.

I opened it without thinking. Inside, wrapped in rustling layers of pink tissue paper, was a pale-blue cotton bra with daisies along the cups and a matching pair of panties. I didn't know what to do. I stood there with them in my hands, feeling my face flush. When I looked up, everyone was looking at me, including Mr. Spence. I avoided Cyril (the little sneak—he must have told her about me trying on hers) and said thank you to Mother. "But . . . how—" I began.

She laughed and sort of sang, "Ah. The man with the set, with the credit! Remember!"

"But, Mother . . ."

"No. Not another word. Try them."

I began to get out of it, but she was so excited and pleased with herself that I didn't have the heart. Sheepishly, I went up to the bathroom and put them on. I told her through the door that the panties were fine, which they were—like thin shorts, really—but she insisted on coming in to check the bra. She fiddled with the straps, raising them up a bit, and tightened the back. Finally she looked me over, with a proud expression on her face. "Perfect," she said. "You see? How much better your profile? And a good fit, no?"

I nodded, a thought about the man with the set idly playing in my head.

When we went downstairs later, Mr. Spence was *still* there. He was just sitting there with the cat on his knee as if he owned the place. (On reflection, I suppose he does own the place.) He said, "Lovely jubbly," at me like he thought he was Jamie Oliver, and I was almost sick.

7 p.m.

Just back from dropping in on Delilah. William had, apparently, dropped in already.

He was sitting on her chair, blue and silver to match her computer desk, kicking off against the floor and swiveling back and forth. Delilah was reclining up on her platform bed; her head at the step end, her dark curls fanning out like Medusa's locks. She had taken off her socks and was trying to touch the stars on the ceiling with her bare toes.

"It's a party!" she said when I came in.

"Your life's one long party," I told her. Then I smelled the incense—Delilah likes to create an atmosphere—and started coughing.

"You okay?" William stopped swiveling when he saw me. I may have imagined it, but I think his eyes flicked momentarily to my new bust.

I crossed my arms. "Bit of a chest, that's all."

William raised his eyes to the ceiling. "Just so long as it's not mono like Julie," he said.

"Is that what she's got?" I said, surprised. "I thought it was tonsillitis."

"Mono's the story going around school."

"Too much kissing," said Delilah.

William and I looked at each other and then looked at her. We both laughed.

"What?"

I pushed the keyboard out of the way and sat on the edge of her desk. "I suppose we're still thinking about your antics last weekend. Have you recovered yet?"

She got up and threw a pillow at me. "Oh, don't," she said. "I've just had all that again from Will."

I ducked the pillow, which tumbled on the desk, knocking over William's tea. He hauled up the pink towel on the floor by his feet and started mopping it. She squealed something about her new Oasis bathrobe and plunged down the platform's steps to pull it out of his hands. There was some jostling and some giggling. I think Delilah may have slapped him around the chest. He dropped the bathrobe and grabbed her wrists.

"Children. Children," I said. Delilah, pink-cheeked and bright-eyed, picked her robe up off the floor. "Hands off my intimates," she said, eyeing William flirtatiously with those big blue eyes of hers. You'd think she was a lady of the night the way she carries on, not some virginal ninth grader from an all-girls' high school.

"Right, I'm off," I said. I uncrossed my arms and stuck my chest out. I'd had enough of this. There were more important things going on in the world. Like war, for one thing. "Coming?" I said to William.

"Owh," said Delilah. "I'll have to do my prep if you go."

"Prep?" William had got up off the chair.

"Fancy girls' homework," I said.

"I'm not fancy!"

"All right. Keep your top on!" He grinned at her.

"Right," I said, and started leaving. Gratifyingly, William followed me down. "See you, then," Delilah called after us, at her door.

Delilah's parents hadn't let William take his bike in— they've got a new oak floor they didn't want scratched— and when we came out, someone had stolen a wheel.

"That'll teach you," I said, and even now I don't know really what I meant.

⅋

In bed, 9 p.m.

Was happily writing the above when I was disturbed by something *awful*. The smell of rose and geranium . . .

Mother was getting out of the bath. "Going out?" I said.

"No. No," she said airily. "Bert's coming around for his lesson."

"BERT!" I yelled. I wasn't expecting to hear *his* name

again. *Ever*. I thought I was on the case. I thought this was something being dealt with. "Here? We still haven't got our kitchen back."

"Ah, well, maybe we'll have takeout, *chérie*."

"Is he paying?" I said.

She looked defensive. "Well, it is my house," she said.

"It's ridiculous. We can't afford it!" The bra straps were digging into my shoulders.

She tutted. "It is not a good time for business," she said. "What with—"

"I know, what with the war."

I stomped downstairs ahead of her to the sitting room. Cyril and Marie were lying on the floor in their pajamas, next to the fridge, wrapped in Mother's duvet.

I hissed, "Ugly Bert is coming around, so you'd better tidy up." I was thinking fast. What could I do to impede this visit?

Marie, who is very impressionable, said, "Ugly Bert. I think he's yuk."

"Unless we can stop him," I said.

Cyril studied me with a curious expression on his face. Marie was drawing a Barbie princess's horse and carriage and didn't seem to notice.

It was six o'clock. I had two hours to put my plan into place. The first thing I did was go upstairs and get into my pajamas and bathrobe (phew: the relief of taking off that bra). Then I came down again and lounged on the sofa bed. Mother was tidying up around the children, putting her clothes into piles, the milk back in the fridge, their scabby toast plates into the sink. "Aghhh," I said after a while. The television was on quite loud and no one noticed. "Aghh," I said again.

Mother looked at me in surprise. I'm very rarely ill. *"Chérie!"* she said. She felt my forehead. "Are you unwell?"

"I don't know. I feel funny," I said.

This piqued Marie's curiosity. She was over like a shot. "Are you going to be sick?" she said.

"I don't know. Aghh."

"If so, can I watch?"

"Marie!" Mother's scold contained a note of alarm. "No. No. I can't have you being sick too."

Then I remembered something. About six months ago, Cyril got some bug and spent a whole night puking. About four in the morning, Marie joined in and Mother assumed she'd caught it too. Suspicions were only raised at breakfast when Marie mysteriously tucked into her cornflakes without a care in the world. I didn't say anything, but I was sure she'd been a victim of sympathy-puke. Some people are more susceptible than others. Marie, whose tastes are finely tuned at the best of times, is *very* susceptible.

"Yes. I do feel sick," I said. "I think it's the smell of the fridge."

"The fridge!" Marie turned to stare at it, still looming over the television.

Mother tutted. "No. No. Not the fridge."

"Yes," I said. "The fridge." Then I gave another bone-vibrating groan.

Mother flapped about, getting me a hot-water bottle. Marie went back to her princess, but kept shooting me, and the fridge, interested glances. Occasionally I would make a gagging motion with my throat and she would quickly look away. I could see her own throat jerk.

"Go to bed if you're not feeling well." Mother got more on edge as 8 p.m. approached. When the doorbell went, she said, "Come on. Up," switched off the TV, and pulled the duvet off Marie and Cyril. Crossly, they both got to their feet just as she let Uncle Bert in. He looked slightly less confident than usual, almost diffident. He made some reference to the builders and the state of the house, and just stood there, a bottle of wine in his hand. Mother was in the doorway saying, "Come on, children. Cyril! Marie!" They began to follow her. I began to panic. But just at that moment, Bert came to my rescue. He was unwrapping the wine from its paper—Californian, I noticed—and touching the side of the bottle with a disgruntled expression on his face. With one pace he crossed to the fridge and, bottle held out, swung it open. I saw my chance, made a lurch with my torso, and let out as loud a gulp as I could muster. Marie spun around. She sniffed. She looked at me. She swallowed. Her eyes glazed. She swallowed again. Her whole body went into spasm and then she was violently, satisfyingly, sick all over Bert's feet. Untapped resource, as I said.

Everything that happened then happened very quickly. Bert, his face screwed up, uttered a succession of horrified noises and disappeared upstairs into the bathroom. Mother, cooing over Marie, who was crying, stripped her of her clothes and then tried to get into the bathroom to wash her down, but couldn't because Bert had locked the door. "Just a minute!" he shouted quite nastily. "I'm cleaning my shoes."

"Yes, but I need to sort out Marie."

"Can't she wait?" he yelled.

Marie was still crying, the poor thing. It's horrible being sick. Guiltily, I could hear her sobs from downstairs, where I had set to with a bucket and cloth. The only thing more horrible than being sick is having anything to do with other people's sick (funny how, no matter what the person's eaten, sick always smells the same), but it was the least I could do. Actually I did start gagging, and had to exert all my powers of control to prevent a little sympathy-puke of my own.

I was on my third bucket of water, careful to breathe through my mouth, not my nose, when Uncle Bert thundered down the stairs, holding his shoes in his hand. "A bag," he said, flicking his blond hair out of his eyes. He had obviously been sponging his trousers, too, because the bottoms were all wet.

"Sorry?"

"A plastic bag. Have you got a plastic bag? For my shoes."

"Um." I got up and rummaged around in the kitchen. All I could find was the stiff cardboard Pritchard & Benning shopping bag from earlier. "This do?"

He grabbed it. "It will have to."

He put his shoes into it and then, his lip curled, pulled off his damp socks, smelled them, and stuffed them in too. I got back on to my hands and knees to finish off. The cat was sniffing around the damp patch in a revolting way. "Hungry?" I said, getting off the floor. "I'll get you some proper food."

"What a to-do!" I said to Bert as I passed him, swinging the bucket in my hand.

He glared at me. "Are you all ill?"

"Just a bug," I said airily.

"What sort of bug?"

"Oh, you know, upset stomach and the runs." I opened a can of KiteKat and started spooning it on to a dish for the cat. "It's going around school. Julie's off sick, as you probably know."

I saw him glance at the cat food and blanch. "I thought that was a throat infection."

I paused. "Oh. Maybe," I said. And then added very quietly, "If that's what they're telling you."

"Oh, Bert. I am so sorry." Mother had come down the stairs, holding Marie's hand. Marie was still shuddering with the aftereffects of tears. "What will you think of us?"

"I'm not sure that I shouldn't head off. You know, you seem to have your hands full."

Mother looked at the wet floor and the bucket filled with swill and gave him a look, which may have contained reproach and may have contained relief. "Maybe," she said.

"Right. Okay. Chickacheet." He kissed her on the head. "Call yer, right?" And he swung out of the sitting room, still dangling the Pritchard & Benning shopping bag from his fingers. He had got to the end of the hall and was halfway out of the door before he remembered us. "Ciao, kids," he yelled before escaping with a slam.

Mother was terribly impressed that I'd cleared up, and very solicitous about my health. After she'd settled Marie, she made me some toast and marmalade. I ate it on the sofa, watching the news. The prime minister was on, looking grave and determined. War has been declared. It really is going to happen now.

I've got a bit stuck in this illness malarkey. I began pretending to feel ill and now I find I actually *do* feel ill. It must be all that shallow breathing and groaning. I expect it restricts the oxygen to your vital organs or something. I'm lying here in bed, all limp and listless. Occasionally I imagine myself jumping out onto the windowsill to see if Delilah's up, or phoning Julie again, but it's too late to do either.

I could be preparing for confession, of course. I've now lost count of my sins. It's awful how one seems to lead to another and each one seems quite valid at the time. It's other people's—in particular Mother's—welfare that is driving me on, after all. It is also astounding how much you can achieve when you put your mind to it. In the past two and a half weeks, I have brought Bert and Mother together and wrenched them apart. The next step—finding her someone else—is bound to be easy. All this and I'm only fourteen. The cat is next to me, and he's purring in approval.

I wonder what the prime minister is thinking. Does he really want a war? Does he think of himself as all-powerful, omnipotent, as being able to do anything he wants? Or is he lying in bed, sick with dread and fear at what might be about to happen next?

Chapter Seventeen

I didn't go to school today. I knew we'd have double French with everyone flashing their latest French-exchange letters about. And I didn't even have to work on an excuse. Mother asked how I was the moment I came down. "Still feeling poorly, *chérie?*" she said, so I only had to nod.

Mr. Spence was sitting at the table in the back bit of the sitting room, drinking tea and eating toast. He seems to get here earlier and earlier. He and Cyril were discussing the relative merits of crunchy versus smooth peanut butter. I heard him say, "I like crunchy on top of ordinary butter, particularly combined with jam, but smooth if I'm just having a cracker. What about you?"

"Same," said Cyril.

Mr. Spence said, "You're just copying." Cyril and

Marie giggled. Honestly, the last thing Mother needs is another child at the table.

"Yeah, well, I think I'd better stay at home today," I said. Mr. Spence and Mother exchanged a glance. I should have seen what was coming. He said, "Well, I'm here all day. So I can tend to the invalid if ness." He was wearing a tight red top with a show-off logo on the shoulder and the kind of narrow jeans Julie calls "ankle-thinners."

I shot Mother a pleading look. "Can't I come to work with you?" I said. "I don't feel ill ill, just sort of not well. But I won't be sick or anything."

She ummed and ahhed. Mr. Spence went into the kitchen and changed into his work clothes. I saw a flash of white leg and royal-blue he-man knickers. Yuk. "Please," I said, shuddering. "I'll be very good. I don't want to be"—I rolled my eyes in his direction (she must know how creepy he is)—"*left.*"

She studied me for a moment, all sorts of thoughts chasing themselves across her face. "Oh. Okay," she said finally. "But be good, huh? Bring a book."

I hadn't realized what a rush it was for her to get C and M to school, catch the train, change at Clapham Junction, and get to work in time for 9:30 a.m. We had to stand all the way too. No wonder her legs ache all the time.

Pritchard & Benning Corsetières is tucked away in a backstreet off a backstreet behind Victoria Station, between a tanning shop and a dry cleaners. It has a very unprepossessing shopfront, and when it's shuttered up, as it was when we arrived, gives no outward indication of the wares inside. It's like something from the olden days. You'd imagine only very ancient and grand ladies totter here to buy eighteen-hour girdles and Cross Your Heart bras. But actually it's very much "on the map," as Mrs. Pritchard puts it. Posh women—or "girls"—flock in their kitten heels from Hampstead and Notting Hill for their expert fittings. It is in certain circles *the only place* to get your bosom measured.

Last time I came was at Christmas, when Jack, the kids, and I collected Mother on our way to see *Puss in Boots* in the West End. We hooted in the street and Mother came flying out. Today Mrs. Pritchard, a great owl of a woman with iron-gray hair and spectacles on a clanking chain around her neck, looked puzzled when she saw me. Mother, hanging up her coat and leaving no room for disagreement, said firmly that I would be "like a little mouse" in the corner. Mrs. Pritchard gave me a tight smile and said if I was good I could help double-check sizes with her in the stockroom. "Well, Bernadette, it looks like you guessed correctly with 34B," she said. "Are you happy with your Lejaby Fantasie, Constance?"

She's so good at her job I hadn't even realized she'd sized me up. I crossed my arms over my chest without thinking. "Yes, thank you," I muttered. I have to say The Bra was a bit more comfortable today.

There are lots of drawers in the stockroom, for each kind of bust, and basically I had to go through them checking they all contained what they should, that no 36EE had slipped into 32C. It didn't take long—there were only a few strays in the lower ranges—and after that I made Mother and Mrs. Pritchard some coffee in the little narrow kitchen behind the stockroom. "How's Mrs. Benning?" I asked Mrs. Pritchard when I brought the cups out. (I'd checked the shop was empty first; she's quite strict about that.)

"Not so good," she said. "Not so good."

I put on a concerned expression. Mrs. Benning has long been a "sleeping partner," but since she went into a nursing home two years ago has done a lot more sleeping than anticipated.

"Oh!" It was about then that Mother let out a little cry. "Look!" She raised her hand as if to wave and then thought better of it. A tall man in a dark suit was walking past the window. "The man with the matching set!"

"The matching set?" I said, momentarily confused.

"You know," she said. "The credit?"

"The credit that your mother so kindly spent on your Lejaby Fantasie matching 34B and Medium," added Mrs. Pritchard, with a small note of reproof.

There are times when I think I am close to sluggish in the speed of my responses, when I despair of my ability ever to grab the moment with the alacrity of, say, Julie. On the other hand, there are times when I amaze even myself.

This was one of those.

"Oh!" I cried. "But I must thank him. I must thank him right now." And I charged out of the shop before anyone could say anything. All I could think was that here was a man who had shown my mother kindness, who we knew was single and who was, if the suit was anything to go by, in regular employment.

"Excuse me!" I shouted after him. He'd reached the corner, but he paused, looking around uncertainly. I panted up. "Sorry." I was still out of breath. "Sorry. Hang on. Phew. My name's Constance and I'm wearing your bra. And—" I had yanked a bit of strap out of my T-shirt but I stopped, registering the alarm on his face. "No. No. That came out wrong. I mean . . . I just wanted to thank you for—"

"For what?" His eyes were darting about in panic, his whole body poised for departure.

"For the Fantasie . . ."

"Good. Good," he said carefully, edging away, as if uncertain of my sanity.

"No. No. Stop. The credit. The shop!" I had his attention and pointed back to Pritchard & Benning, outside of which Mother and Mrs. Pritchard were now standing, looking after us.

"The shop?" he said, still uncertainly, but less wary now.

"Do you remember? A few weeks ago? The credit?"

"The credit?"

"You know. The matching set you bought for your fiancée, 'big on top, tiny down below,' the fiancée that then broke it off . . ."

"Oh. The credit." He looked sad. "Oh. I see."

"It was so very kind. My mother, *a widow*, has had such a tough time recently. And an act of generosity like yours . . . well . . . it made her week. Her month! But, of course, being the sweet person she is, she spent it on me. On my bosoms. I mean, she bought me a bra! And, well, I just wanted to thank you. And I know that she'd like to thank you herself. So, I mean, if you had a minute and could spare the time just to return to the shop so that she could do that, well . . ."

He looked at me as if he still thought I was barking, but then looked again down the road to where Mother was standing, her hands held at her tiny waist, her rosebud mouth twisting, the light playing with her shiny dark hair. She looked gamine and beautiful.

He nodded—as I've said before, Mother does have that effect—and followed me.

Mother looked less unsure and more cross when we reached her. She said, "Constance!" but I jumped in quickly.

"Mother, we wanted to thank Mr.— Sorry, I don't know your name—"

"Savonaire." The man and I both looked at Mother after she'd spoken. She added quickly, "It was on the credit."

He smiled. "Victor Savonaire," he said, and put out his hand for both of us to shake it.

I heard myself breathe rather than say, "You're French." (It was the way he'd pronounced *Victor* that clinched it.)

"My mother," he said. "So, half French, yes. But born and brought up in London, so a bit of a mix, I'm afraid." Until then I hadn't been sure about his looks. He was slim and tall, not thin, but his face was bony. He had nice eyes but rather too prominent eye sockets. And something odd was going on on the top of his head. There was pale-brown hair, tufting upward as if gelled, but not as much as there should have been. Someone was hiding something. Still, *half French*! You could forgive some follicular fudging for that!

Mother began asking whether he was feeling, er, better since their last meeting. He looked down at the pavement and kicked the dust about with his shiny shoes as he answered. His voice was very fancy, but faltering.

Mother said, "I was worried, as I remarked to you at the time, that our choice of lingerie had not been appropriate, that it might have made the situation worse."

He said, "No, no. I mean, rather, yes, but no. It was more that she was already confused and a gift of that nature reminded, or rather not reminded but . . ." And he trailed away.

I looked from one to the other of them. Mother had on her sick-child expression. I could see she was just longing to get out the Calpol and wrap him in her duvet on the sofa. And he—well, I don't know. But he didn't have to stand there talking to her, did he?

I could see Mrs. Pritchard peering out at us over Mother's shoulder. And then a taxi drew up and a couple of women carrying the kind of logoed handbags that look like miniature suitcases got out and started tottering toward the shop.

"Oh," said Mother. "It was charming to meet you and, once again, thank you for your act of generosity." She smiled and turned and, following the women with the mini luggage, went back into the shop.

Victor Savonaire continued to stand there for a second, looking dazed. At the time, I assumed it was bewilderment at Mother's beauty, though as I sit here writing, it strikes me that maybe it was the churning up of

Valentine's Day memories, the one minute walking along the pavement, the next forced into an intimate conversation, that threw him. But it doesn't matter. If I was deluded, so be it. It gave me confidence to do what I did next and confidence, as I'm beginning to see, is what matters in life.

"Right," he said. "Okay. Well, thank you, or rather thank you for thanking me, and for . . ."

"Come to tea."

"What?"

"On Saturday. Come to tea."

His mouth dropped open and one of his hands shot to the top of his head, where the fingers twiddled vaguely for a moment before falling to scratch behind his ears.

I fired out our address. "Please," I said. "We would so like to thank you. I'll make a cake."

He ummed and ahhed but finally, hesitantly, said he would. I wrote our address down on the back of his hand. Then we said good-bye and I went back into the shop.

Mother was in and out of the fitting room with armfuls of small boxes, dancing attendance on one of the women from the taxi, and could only look at me suspiciously. Then Mrs. Pritchard sent me out for some tea bags. And then there was a flood of second-wind shoppers (customers buying bras to go with the outfits they'd bought in the morning), so it wasn't until much later in the afternoon that I had to 'fess up. I'm afraid I wasn't completely honest. I'd had time to prepare a tiny little embellishment to make it sound more plausible. I told her he'd said, "It would be nice to meet again in more auspicious circumstances," and that I'd felt it would have been rude not to arrange something after that. Her brown eyes widened. I said, "And so tea seemed the most harmless, don't you think?"

"Er." She laughed, more in shock than anything. "You really invited him to tea, Connie?"

"Yup."

She laughed again. Actually, I don't think she believed me yet. "When again?"

"Saturday."

"And how does he know where we live?"

"I told him."

"And, Connie—" She was standing with her hands on her hips. "What about your job at the drugstore?"

I'd forgotten that. But it didn't throw me. "Well," I said boldly, "I suppose you'll have to entertain him until I get there."

I'm in bed—exhausted. It's been a busy day for an ill person. I only have one more thing to recount and that's that I did manage to speak to Julie before I came to bed. Her mom, who answered the phone, said I could talk to her as long as I was quick and didn't ask too many questions. "She'd like to hear your voice, I'm sure," she said.

Julie came on and said something in a tiny whisper that I decoded as "hello."

"Is it mono?" I said.

"Tonsillitis," she whispered. "Thank God."

"What a relief." I added lots of sympathetic things and then, "So we're doing brilliantly on the anti–Uncle Bert campaign."

She uttered a painful high squeaking noise that I took for encouragement.

"Yes. And well done you for last Sunday. Don't know what you did, but it worked."

She gave another squeak.

"Though I've had to be quite busy since. Marie puked up all over him and I think that really put him off. And now I'm hard at work finding Mother another man." And then I told her all about Victor Savonaire.

She gave a terrible strangulated laugh that turned into a cough. I think she croaked "Leakey The Pharmacist?" But then her mom took the phone from her.

"That's enough for tonight, Connie," she said. "I'm sure she'll be back next week. You can catch up with each other then. Thanks for calling."

So that's that. I'm on my own for now. And I'm not doing too badly.

PS Isn't Savonaire a heavenly name? Like fancy soap.

Chapter Eighteen

I got up really, really early and I've been frantically busy ever since. Full of hope and expectation. And other more confused emotions, of which more later.

I've left the house all ready. There is a cake, plump and sweet, sitting in the ice-cream carton we use as a tin in the kitchen. I dusted it with sugar, so it would look like the kind of cake they have in French patisseries. (Julie and I spent a lot of time in French patisseries on the day trip to Boulogne.) There are cucumber sandwiches— Victor Savonaire definitely looks like a cucumber-sandwich man—covered in the fridge. And there is a tray ready laid, complete with teapot, cups, and milk jug (the one Marie decorated with kangaroos at one of those do-it-yourself pottery places. Or I think they're kangaroos. They might be cows).

When I showed Mother what I'd done she said, "*Mon ange.*" She was a bit distracted because Marie and Cyril were fighting over the plastic dinosaur that came in a new package of corn pops. I hope she remembers to sift the sugar.

I walked to work feeling very organized and bossy, omnipotent like a Roman emperor, or the matriarch of some large ungainly family, like in the Mafia or something. I was unbeatable. I keep thinking how impressed Julie will be with me.

I was brought down to earth before I got to the drugstore, because I met William in front of the station. He was waiting for his brother and he seemed to be in a bad mood.

"Where're you off to?" I said. "Soccer? Away match in some hellhole end of the universe?"

"Nope," he said, scowling. He had a little scrap of toilet paper stuck just below his ear. "No, Kevin wants to go on the march today. You know, in the park?"

I did know. I'd seen it on the news—there's been bombing in the last few days; a lot of buildings blown up, some casualties—but Victor Savonaire had put it out of my mind.

"That's good," I said, noticing that William looked quite handsome now his hair was growing out a little bit. Mind you, it needed a wash.

"No, it's not." He rubbed his hand across his nose (*not* attractive). "We're away at Arsenal. I want to go to that. And what's the point of marching? What difference will we make? It's all happening too far away. It's nothing to do with us. It's pointless."

I was still thinking about that when I arrived at the shop. John Leakey was behind the counter, looking cross.

"So your mom's boyfriend's happy?" he said when he saw me.

I didn't immediately grasp what he meant. I must have just stared at him blankly.

"A show of might and all that." He gestured to a new poster in the window. It was advertising the march in the park. "Troublemaking, I'm afraid. Some of us feel it's not a good thing seeing innocent people die. Let alone the knock-on effect on business or whatever it was." His beetle brows seemed to meet in the middle.

"I know," I said. "Awful." But I didn't really mean it. I was thinking how magnificent some people look when they're angry.

He stared at me. "Yes," he said quietly. "Yes, it is." He gave his head a little shake and then said, "Right. Sorry. Connie, can you and Gail manage this morning? I've got Sanjay, the substitute pharmacist, coming in. I'm off to—"

"The march?" I said, gesturing to the poster.

He nodded. "Yup. Sorry. I just think it's important to

make a stand. You know, when you believe in something strongly."

I nodded. "Of course." I got my overall on and picked up the price gun.

But I couldn't concentrate. I'd forgotten about the war. I'd been so determined to watch the news and follow it. And I haven't, really. Not a lot. My own life has taken over. It's all begun to seem such a long way away—like William said—and nothing to do with me. Also, worst of all, I did see the news last night and I did see the bombs go off, but I'd been too busy worrying about Victor Savonaire's cake to think any more about it.

After a while I said, "Mr. Leakey, I mean John?"

"Yes?"

"I think you're so good to go on the march. I think you're magnifi— remarkable, really. You know, to care and to notice and . . ."

He didn't look up from his accounts. "You have to make a stand."

"Even if it doesn't make a difference? Even if it isn't the right thing? I mean, how do you know whether a war is a good thing or a bad thing?"

He looked up now. "That, Connie, you have to work out for yourself. You mustn't listen to me, or your mom's boyfriend. You have to work it out for yourself. It's that simple."

"I know." I priced a few more toothpaste tubes and then stopped again. I wanted to tell him something—something really awful—and I was worried that if I did he wouldn't like me anymore. But I also knew that he would listen. There is something so understanding about him. He takes you seriously, even if you're only fourteen.

"Mr. Leakey? John? You know last night, the bombing? I saw it, and the houses being destroyed, and I knew there were real people in the houses who were being killed, but it's only now, talking to you, that I sort of realize they are people like you and me. They didn't seem—" Could I tell him? "They didn't seem as real somehow. Do you know what I mean?"

He'd been working on the other side of the counter to me, but when I said this he came around and leaned against the shelves just by me. "That's very honest of you." He considered for a while. "It's very easy to feel that. It's like watching a film. It can even be exciting. That's why war is a dangerous thing. It's desensitizing. It becomes something other than it is, which is everyday and brutal."

I nodded, but I didn't look up. I felt shy suddenly because he was so close. He took my hand and squeezed it. His grasp felt firm and warm. His breath smelled of tea and mints. He said, "Connie, at sixteen, you have to start listening to other people and drawing your own conclusions. Don't just follow the crowd, or me."

"At sixt—" I began. I looked up and then remembered. Our eyes met. His lashes are so long you'd think they'd get tangled. I felt this weird tight feeling in my stomach, like butterflies and nausea muddled up, the feeling you get at the back of your throat when you've been running fast, or biking, but it wasn't in my throat, it was farther down in the depths of my chest, like everything was taut.

I laughed to cover my embarrassment and said, "Anyway, the good news is he's not her boyfriend anymore."

"Who isn't?" He had returned to the register as if nothing had happened.

"My mom's boyfriend isn't my mom's boyfriend anymore."

He looked up from the roll of receipts he'd been studying and laughed. "That's good, then, isn't it? Because we don't like him, do we?"

I laughed too. He was back on the other side of the counter, but for a moment there, it was him and me against the world. "No," I said, "we don't."

&

Drugstore counter, 4 p.m.

The time is dragging really slowly. Sanjay, a studious lad straight out of college, is keeping himself to himself out

~ 153 ~

the back. The only time we talk is when I say, "Nurofen!," holding up a box, and he nods. When it's busy, Gail tends to get quite flustered. But when it's quiet she taps the stool next to her and says, "Come and perch yourself down here." Today she wanted to know how I was getting on with my "BF," whether things were okay between us now. I forgave the "BF"—it's her attempt to sound streetwise even if her street does lead to some jolly-hockey-sticks school of the fifties. I told her everything between me and my "BF' was hunky-dory.

I asked after her mother, who is "bearing up" in the hospital, we sold some whitening toothpaste, and then she said, "And your young man, all well there?"

"What young man?" I answered.

"The one on the bike, who spends the whole of Saturday afternoon biking up and down outside the shop, pretending not to look in."

"He doesn't!" I looked out of the window, but the street was empty.

"He does," she said in a singsong voice. "Though I haven't seen him yet today."

"That's because he's gone to the march."

"Told you so!" She thought she'd caught me out.

"He's not my young man," I insisted. "He's just a friend. I don't even—"

"What?" She was laughing at me.

I looked over my shoulder to check that Sanjay wasn't listening. "I don't even like him. He's not my type." (What *is* my type? Also, what's William playing at? Why's he spying on me?)

I wonder what's happening at home. Victor Savonaire should be there now. I hope Mother remembered the icing sugar. I hope they're having fun. Maybe they've finished tea and have moved on to wine. (French, I bet. There's nothing gay New World about *him*.)

⅋

5 p.m.

Off home now. I can't wait to see how things have gone.

⅋

Halfway to Richmond, 7 p.m.

Oh, woe.

I'm on the bus on my way to visit Julie with a heavy heart.

I opened the door very noisily—in case Mother and Victor Savonaire needed warning—but I needn't have bothered. The sitting room was empty. So was the kitchen. Worse. On the counter was the tea tray, just as I'd left it. I opened the ice-cream carton to find an *uncut cake*. And in the fridge, twinkling defiantly out at me from beneath their wrapper, was a pile of *uneaten cucumber sandwiches.* Wrong. One corner had been disturbed. A pile of uneaten cucumber sandwiches *minus one.*

There was a sound upstairs.

"Mother!" I yelled.

"*Chérie!*" tinkled her voice from the bathroom. "How was your da-ay?"

I stuffed my earnings into the cookie jar and went upstairs. The bathroom door was open. There was rose and geranium in the air, so there was still hope. "What's happened?" I said, bursting in.

Mother was in the bath. "I'm so glad you're back," she said, craning, when she saw me. "Little Julie has called. She would so like you to go and see her this evening. At last she is better. I'm glad to see you before I go."

"You're going out?" I said.

"In a few instants, yes. Now, Jack will be bringing Cyril and Marie back at eight o'clock. You can get the bus to Julie's, no?"

"Yes. Yes. Okay. But what happened? The cake? The tea?"

"Oh." She took a sharp intake of breath. "Constance, after all that trouble you went to. That man didn't come at all. I was waiting and no—nothing. But I had a sandwich. They were very nice."

"You mean he didn't turn up?"

"No." She sounded offended, in a high-horse kind of a way, but not upset. "He didn't turn up at all."

I pulled the toilet lid down and sat on it. "I don't understand. He said he would come. I gave him the address."

She shrugged and reached for the soap. "Men," she said.

I stood up. I had to call Julie and tell her I was coming straight away. She would know what to do. I needed advice. Input. I was halfway out of the door when I thought to ask Mother where she was going.

She checked her watch, which was on the side of the bath by her head, and made to get up. "I'm just going for a quick drink with Bert," she said.

I nearly died.

⅋

Bedroom, 10:30 p.m.

Julie, apparently, *has* nearly died. "Daggers," she said. "My throat felt like daggers. Now it's more . . ."

"Chopsticks?" I suggested.

"Yes. Or toothpicks. You wearing a bra?" she added.

"Yep."

"Big improvement."

Julie's mom had made a real fuss of me at the door, telling me how thrilled Julie would be to see me. And she *was* thrilled. She'd been at the window, in her River Island daywear cotton drawstrings and a frilly T-shirt—and she did a Tiggerlike bounce back into bed when I came in. "Company," she croaked. "Friendship. News from the great outdoors."

"Also homework," I said, handing her a copy of the previous week's assignments (which she promptly chucked on to the bedside table).

There were flowers by the bed, too, daffodils and baby's breath. "Who're they from?" I asked.

"Ade!"

"Ade?"

"The guy from the party. Just before I got ill." She wriggled her shoulders. "He's so sweet. He keeps calling. He brought these around, though Mom wouldn't let him up. Luckily. Look at the state of me. He's not embarrassed to show he cares. It's so totally sexy."

Her mom came in then, with two cups of tea. "Thanks, Mom," she whispered in a little-girl-lost voice.

"You," her mom said, "are well enough to get your own next time."

Now she was leaning back against the pillows, with the duvet tucked over her. She looked younger without her heavy black eyeliner. Despite the vase of flowers on her bedside table, the room had that musty closed-in smell of illness, of breath and skin and stale flower water.

Balls of tissue decorated the carpet like giant confetti. A copy of *Sneak* magazine and a novel with a cartoon girl in a pink miniskirt and thigh-high boots on the front lay abandoned on the bedside table.

"Gossip," Julie said when her mom had gone again. "Scandal. Tell me everything. What's been going on while I've been stuck here at death's door?"

"I've got news," I said grimly. I took a deep breath and told her everything. I told her about bad-mouthing Uncle Bert, about scrumpling up his phone message. I told her about taking the day off from school and accosting Victor Savonaire. I told her about the preparations for tea. I told her about Victor Savonaire not deigning to turn up. And finally I told her about Mother's "quick aperitif" that evening.

Her expression went from glee to mild disapproval to encouragement to excitement to disappointment—to horror. "Uncle Bert's taking her out again?" she croaked. "Tonight? I thought you said on the phone you'd split them up?"

"I thought I had too."

"I thought you'd sorted everything."

"I know. I know. I thought I had too."

Her mouth went into a hard line. "Right," she growled. "Where's that list?"

"That list?"

"You know, the matchmaking list." Her voice was really going now. "The one we made right at the beginning."

I produced the page in this book where it's reproduced. "Now—business. Hah! Monsieur Baker."

"No." I remembered the nipples through the thin white shirt. "Please."

"We're not talking stepfather material. We're talking get us out of this fix."

"No," I said again.

"Okay." Her eyes scanned the page, then, "Aha! What are we thinking? It's here! The answer's here! It's obvious and the beauty of it is it's all set up. You've set it up already, you brilliant thing."

"What?" I bent to pick up a tissue off the floor by my feet. But I think I already knew.

"The Pharmacist!"

"No." I felt my face go wooden. "We can't do that."

"Why ever not? Con, it's perfect. You're already in there. Remember, it's why you started working there in the first place. A backup! Now we need it. And by this stage in the game, he knows you. You know him. It'll be easy. All you have to do is invite him around."

"It's not fair," I replied. I was pulling the tissue to pieces, scattering paper petals all over the bed. "It's . . . it's . . . not right."

"I thought you liked him?"

"I do. . . ."

"Well, there"—her voice was beginning to fade and she took a glug of tea to bring it back—"you go."

I couldn't think of any concrete reasons to say no. I said there were no French connections. She said I was being too fussy. I tried to say more about how having got to know John ("John?" she interrupted. "Mr. Leakey," I corrected.) made me feel uncomfortable about it. She said *she* knew Uncle Bert: that hadn't stopped her. Wasn't it better to be working with people we knew than with people, like my Savonaire bloke, who might be half French but who didn't even turn up when you'd gone to the trouble of making cucumber sandwiches? In the end I found myself agreeing. "Arrange something fast," she croaked. "We don't want another disaster like today."

I feel troubled. I don't want to let Julie down—again—and I do want to find a new man for Mother and stop her seeing Uncle Bert. But I'm just not sure John Leakey is right. He is nice, really nice, and he talks to people my age like they're ordinary humans, not creatures from Planet Zog. I've seen him give small kids free lollies too—and not look cross when he has to get the jar down again to let them swap their banana one for a strawberry one. He's gentle and clever and good-looking and, as Julie also reminded me tonight, he's got a great arse. I just can't see him with Mother. I don't know why. But the thought of it makes my stomach do funny, panicky things.

I've got Julie's face in my head, her eyes pleading with me. Her eyes are lined with black kohl, whereas this evening they were makeup free, and I realize I'm remembering her as she was the other day when she came to meet me at the drugstore. And I'm remembering how horrible it was when she and Carmen had their backs to me on the radiator at school and how left out I felt, and how wonderful it was when I realized it was only Uncle Bert that was stopping us from being friends. But am I letting her manipulate me? Is William right that she likes things her own way? Oh God, what am I on about? Friendship is just *so hard*.

I got home at 9 p.m. and Mother got back at about 10 p.m.—so not a long aperitif at all. She was in a thoughtful mood, which I took as a good sign. Or not a bad sign, at least.

We watched the news together and ate the rest of the cucumber sandwiches. More bombing. More politicians. And 200,000 people marching through the streets of London. That's 199,999 people. And John Leakey. My pharmacist.

Chapter Nineteen

TUESDAY, MARCH 11
*Kitchen (hooray: complete with
roof and fridge!), 5 p.m.*

I did it. I dropped in today on the way back from
school. Luckily the shop was empty. John was doing
something with the photo processor; he'd dismantled it
and had all the bits on the floor around him. He grunted
when he saw me. "Jammed," he said. "It's eaten Mrs.
Rayburn's Women's Institute trip to Salisbury Cathedral.
Twenty-four exposures wiped out in one."

"Could have been worse," I said. "Could have been
Mrs. Rayburn's once-in-a-lifetime safari in Tanzania."

He laughed, but as he was still frowning at the time,
it came out like a "harumph."

He jigged the contraption back together. When he
stood up, there was black stuff on his hands. He bent to
wipe them on a paper towel. He was wearing his jeans.
"Did I underpay you or something?"

"What?"

"Midweek visit. We're honored." He seemed to have noticed something odd about me, because he was giving me a funny look. Then he said, "Didn't know your school wore uniforms as juniors."

"It's not a uniform and I'm not a junior!" I was outraged. Under my jacket, I was wearing a pale-blue Aertex shirt (fifty pence) and a dark-gray pleated skirt (twenty pence, bargain bucket), which I felt suited me rather well.

"You're not a junior?"

I'd been so insulted by his attack on my clothes-sense, I'd completely forgotten about *all that*, the deception on which our relationship was founded. It's why you should never lie. People say you're always caught out in the end, as if a lie grows and grows over time, rolling down the road after you, collecting debris until it's so *huge* it can't be ignored any longer. But actually it gets smaller and smaller, shrinking to something so tiny and inconsequential that it slips through a gap without you noticing.

"Ah," I said. "What I mean is, I am, but I don't. Yes. Um. Well, you don't have to. You don't have to every day."

"You mean it is a uniform, but you don't have to wear it? It's a question of choice?"

"Yup. Yup. That's it."

His expression as he looked at me got even odder. I pulled in the belt of my pack-a-mac a bit tighter. I found my hands fiddling at my neck. "You're a funny girl," he said eventually.

"Anyway. The reason I'm here is to see if you'd like to come to my house for supper," I said.

"Connie!" He looked astonished. I think his cheeks may have gone a bit pink. "Are you worried I'm not eating?"

"No. No. Well, you could eat something other than bacon sandwiches. But no. It's just . . . well, I was talking about the job, my job here, with my mother, Bernadette, and she said how nice it would be to meet you properly. I mean, I know she's been in once or twice. . . ."

"Has she?" He looked puzzled. "I don't remember. Oh yes! The lady with the beehive."

"The beehive? No. No, that's Granny Enid. My step-grandmother." I smiled at the thought of how different Mother was to Granny Enid; what a surprise he'd get if that was what he was expecting. "I suppose she hasn't been in much since I've been working here. I can buy what she needs. Which reminds me." I had a sudden inspiration and turned to the shelves. I pulled out a bottle and brandished it. "She's about to run out of Neutrogena T/Gel Anti-Dandruff Shampoo!"

He ran it up on the register.

I said, "Yup. Neutrogena T/Gel Anti-Dandruff Shampoo. She lives on the stuff."

He still looked unfazed. Had he forgotten the valentine card? "Four pounds thirty," he said.

I rummaged in my pocket. "Oh," I said. "Actually, I haven't got enough. Perhaps I'll get it on Saturday."

"You sure?" he said.

"Yeah. No problem." I laughed. "So. Ms Neutrogena T/Gel Anti-Dandruff Shampoo, that's what they call her."

"Who?"

"My mother." He looked at me blankly. I gave up. "So, will you?"

"Er . . ."

"Come to supper?"

He made a face, which I couldn't read. "Yes. Okay," he said. "When?"

"I was thinking tomorrow?" (Mother never goes out on Wednesdays. She watches *ER*.)

"Let me just consult my hectic social calendar." He tipped his head back, closed his eyes for a second, and then opened them. "Actually, I appear to have a cancellation tomorrow. I did have plans with Victoria Beckham and Tara Palmer-Tomkinson—just a bacon sandwich around my place; always Tara's date of choice—but they've come down with chicken flu. So—amazingly, considering the short notice—I'm free."

"Good. Eight o'clock. You've got the address, haven't you?"

"I have. And, to eat, will it be—?"

"Fish. Yes, I expect it will."

He wrinkled his nose. "Just so long as it's freshly delivered from Newcastle, that'll be fine."

I don't think I've ever got on with an adult as well as I get on with John.

The good news back in our house is that Mr. Spence has finally finished redecorating the kitchen. The bad news is that he has started on the bathroom. I could hear him singing as I opened the front door. "'It's fun to stay at the YMCA,'" he was yodeling like some over-ebullient goatherd. I needed to pee, so I went in. The window was wide open and strips of peeled wallpaper lay over the bath like drunken maidens. He was up a ladder, scraping the ceiling. "Would you mind giving me a few minutes to myself?" I said haughtily.

"Wotcha!" he said, climbing down the ladder.

I gave him a withering look. And then I shut the bathroom door in his face.

⅋

My room, 7 p.m.

I've just told Mother about John Leakey coming to supper. I want to thank him, I said, for giving me the job. "That's sweet," she said. "So I can leave you to it and watch *ER?*" I told her she couldn't, that she'd have to tape it. Then I felt odd about it all. I am doing the right thing, aren't I?

I've just called Julie. "Connie," she said, "you're a star."

Chapter Twenty

WEDNESDAY, MARCH 12
The farthest reaches of my wardrobe,
7:45 p.m.

I'm getting quite good at this hostess malarkey. Obviously my dream is to go to France and become part of the Parisian literary scene, to smoke a lot and wear a beret. But if I can't do that, I could always go into catering. With fifteen pounds from the cookie jar I have bought three chicken breasts, a bag of tiny potatoes, a large package of ready-washed salad, a jar of mushroom sauce, and a treacle tart. Oh, and a box of chocolate-chip cookies to console Cyril and Marie, because they've had to go to bed early. I was thinking of a way to get wine, but that bottle of white is still in the fridge from Bert's abortive puke visit. New World, but can't be wasted.

Mr. Spence was stripping the bathroom when I got in from school. I went in—twice—to warn him that we are having company and to make sure he was "all tidied up" before Mother gets home. By "all tidied up," of course, I meant "got the hell out." He said, "Okey-dokey, chokey lokey," and ruffled my hair like we were the best of friends. I smoothed it down immediately.

I said tartly, "It's beginning to look like you're going to be working in our house forever." I think he got the message because, unusually for him, he left before Mother arrived. Hooray.

I've just spent a good half an hour in front of the mirror trying to work out what to wear. Something odd seems to have happened to my clothes. They all look moth-eaten and dowdy, or downright weird. Do I really wear that yellow shirt under the green velvet pinafore? Or that dull "school" skirt (John's right) with the stripy tights? Just now, I long for something more elegant. I tried on some of Mother's work clothes—the black skirt and roll neck that make her look so chic. But I couldn't do up the skirt, and the roll neck made me look like a sack of puppies.

I looked at myself in my underwear. I've got red and white blotches on my thighs and my tummy sticks out. My legs are all right. I wish I had smaller boobs. My bra, my Fantasie, seems to draw attention to them. I'm aware of them in a way I never used to be. They are just *there*. They're like a whole new part of me; they get everywhere first. And other people seem to notice them too. I even saw Joseph Milton looking at them the other day. I had to whack him with my bag.

In the end I've put on my paisley ski pants and a pink T-shirt. I've been experimenting with one of Mother's old eyeshadows I found in the bathroom. I look awful. Like a raccoon with a hangover.

Oh, lordy. Time is moving on. He'll be here soon.

I got my instructions from Julie at school today. Do camouflage the rug rats. Don't hog the conversation. Do go to the loo for long periods of time to give them a chance to talk. Don't let him leave early. Do put on romantic music. Do go to bed early myself.

I've plumped up the sofa-bed cushions. I've laid the table. I've dusted the TV. The food's ready . . . Mother's set the tape for *ER*, but she hasn't changed. She hasn't had a rose-and-geranium bath either. She's very relaxed about it all, unlike me! Oh, I wish I didn't feel so nervous.

Doorbell. *Help!*

ক

My bedroom, 11:30 p.m.

I've left my door open and I can hear the occasional peal of laughter above the music. The CD seems to be on repeat and no one has noticed. I should get into my pajamas, but I can't stay still. I can't go to bed until he leaves. They've both got work tomorrow. This can't go on much longer.

He looked twitchy when he arrived, handing me a bottle of wine—not New World, but French!—and a foursome of Cokes, and sort of peering in past me like he was worried what he might find. He had on different jeans from the ones he had on in the shop; these were stonewashed in places, dark blue with artificially faded grooves across the thighs and knees. And he was wearing a black leather jacket over a thin black polo-neck sweater, which I didn't really like. I think he needs light, or bright, colors to compensate for the darkness of his coloring. Not that I said anything, of course.

Mother was washing up the children's fish-finger plates and came out, drying her hands on a tea towel. She looked taken aback when she saw him. I suppose she might have been expecting someone much older, like Mr. Leakey senior, retired. I introduced them, and they shook hands. A little while later, Mother went upstairs to check on M and C, and when she came down, she'd refreshed her lipstick.

It was a bit awkward at first. From the kitchen, where I was fiddling about with the grill pan, trying not to set light to the chicken breasts, I could hear faltering attempts at conversation, to do with retail and market forces. At one point I heard them talking about me—my "maturity" (yikes). But then she, not very subtly, went over to check the video and he asked what she was tap-ing and she said, "*ER*," and he said, "But I love *ER*," and before I knew it (which was actually after quite a bit of time as the chicken didn't seem to be quite cooking *through*), they had sat down together to watch it. When the meal was finally ready, Mother asked if they could have it on a tray and I got quite snippy. "I've laid the table," I said. After that, it all went with a buzz. He wasn't grumpy like he can be. He told lots of jokes and did impressions of some of his customers. He didn't even look annoyed when the conversation came around to the war and Mother said she thought those pictures of the injured and dead people looked "manufactured." He simply said, "Well, I don't know. The pictures may be used as propaganda, but that doesn't mean the bombing didn't happen." And she shrugged, but not rudely, more as if perhaps she agreed, after all.

I'd still be down there if it wasn't for Julie. She called during supper. "You still up?" she hissed.

I was still laughing from John's impression of the Zantac drug rep. "Yeah," I said. "Supper was rather late in the end."

"Well, you shouldn't still be there. Go to bed. Leave them."

"But—" John hadn't stopped for my phone call. He was opening an invisible briefcase with the self-important flourish of a cabinet minister. Mother had thrown back her head to laugh. "It's early. It's only—"

"Ten thirty. Bugger off."

"But we haven't had dessert."

"Connie." There was a warning in her voice.

I felt my knees go weak. "Okay."

I went back to the table. Mother's feet were resting on my empty seat. She moved them out of the way when she saw me, but I didn't sit down. I poured them both another glass of wine (they'd drunk Bert's white and were on John's red) and said I was turning in. John stood up to see me off. He thanked me for inviting him, said what a change chicken à la mushroom made from bacon sandwiches, and, checking his watch, said he should be heading off himself.

"But"—there was something hard in the back of my throat preventing the words from running smoothly—"you haven't had your dessert yet. It's . . . it's treacle tart."

"I'm too full," said Mother languidly from the table.

I snapped, "I bought it for John."

I saw her incline her head very slightly. John widened his soft brown eyes a fraction, then laughed. "Treacle tart," he said. "My favorite. Well, if you're not longing to get rid of me . . . Maybe we could take our bowls and watch the end of *ER*?"

Mother nodded her agreement. So I got their treacle

tarts and kissed Mother to say sorry for being short with her. Then I came up here.

That was *hours* ago! Or an hour anyway. And since then I've been pacing the room, pausing to strain my ears at the door to see if I can pick up what they're saying, then pacing over to the window, then to the bed, then back to the door. I'm feeling weird, left out and resentful, grumpy and anxious. My head feels as if there are drill holes all over it. My eyes ache. It seems wrong that John, who is *my* boss, after all, should be downstairs on his own with Mother. I think maybe he's too young for her. Isn't he closer to my age? There's another giggle. What's he saying now that's so funny? They've hit it off, haven't they? It's worked. But I wish they'd be quiet. Some of us have school tomorrow.

I know what the problem is. It's . . . it's *unprofessional.*

Chapter Twenty-one

*M*other hasn't said much about John since last night. I thought she would be full of him at breakfast, but she was too busy chatting to Mr. Spence about *his* evening. (He'd gone to the greyhounds, which—"ooh la la"—she seemed to find fascinating.) The washing up was still in the sink from the night before: the grill pan with the bits of chicken suspended in cold fat, the pot with the dried-up mushroom sauce. I tried to show my irritation by washing up loudly and sighing in an exasperated way. But no one seemed to notice. Mr. Spence had moved on from greyhounds and was making silly Donald Duck noises for Marie.

Then Mother, who was putting her mascara on at the kitchen counter, said, "Constance had her first little dinner party last night. Which is why she wanted you out of the house!"

He said, "Oh, I see," in a rather meaningful way and looked relieved, which he had no right to. Mother must have seen my expression because then she said, "And very nice it was, too," and gave a little laugh. Mr. Spence laughed too. And then they went upstairs to discuss the new tiles in the bathroom and they were still doing that when William called for me.

I told Julie all about it at school. "A triumph, then!" she said. And she started talking about Ade, the big love of her life, which has survived even her illness. "He's not afraid to show he cares," Julie says. I would have thought it would put her off, but it hasn't. On the way home I bumped into Delilah, who is gearing up for her party. She's asked William—"dear Will"—to walk her home and he's said he will. Fool.

Everything was normal this evening until about 8:30 p.m. when the phone rang. Mother answered it. I didn't think much of it—I was about to take M and C up for bath and bed—but when I came back down again half an hour later, she was *still on the phone*. She was curled up in one corner of the sofa, with her feet tucked under her, and her head back, and she was talking softly and laughing from time to time. I made her some tea, which she acknowledged with a slight tilt of her head, but she didn't hang up. When I put the TV on, she went through into the kitchen. Finally I came up here. *And she's still on it.*

I could have sworn I heard her say "John."

Chapter Twenty-two

FRIDAY, MARCH 14
Kitchen, 10 p.m.

Mother came back earlier than usual today with a
big bag under her arm and a big grin on her face. She'd
bought herself a new dress "to wear tonight." It's been
raining since four o'clock—big, wet, horizontal rain that
drenches you in seconds. She came in the front door
bedraggled, like a half-drowned black cat, but she was
laughing and singing, "'I'm singin' and dancin' in the
rain.'" Her eyelashes sparkled with raindrops. She
dipped her head forward and shook it, so that droplets
ricocheted on to the floor. She didn't stop laughing
until she'd stripped off all her clothes and got into her
big terrycloth bathrobe. Then she hugged me. "Cheer up,
chicken," she said.

"Going somewhere special?" I said, gesturing at
the bag.

She dragged the chair into the middle of the sitting room and stood up on it, holding the garment in front of the bathrobe and preening. She got down and sat on the edge of the sofa, folding the dress on to her knee.

"Maybe," she said. "Yes, maybe."

She looked at me and gave a little smile. Then she patted the seat next to her. "Come," she said, "*chérie.*"

"What?" I said in a sulky voice. I didn't know what was wrong with me.

"I am feeling happy," she said once I'd sat down. "I have a date tonight and I am excited."

"Is it Bert?" I said.

She laughed. "Bert? No. That was nothing. It was French lessons. Bert! No."

I should have felt relief, but I didn't. "Victor Savonaire?" I said, clutching at straws.

She shook her head and frowned.

"Who, then?" I said, my tongue heavy in my mouth.

"You don't know?"

"No."

"You haven't guessed?"

"No."

"It's someone you know," she said teasingly. "The other night, your little supper, it triggered—"

"So it's John?" I said.

There was a pause before she answered. A dreamy

look came into her eyes, rather like Delilah when she's imagining Mr. Right. Then she nodded. "Yes," she said. "Yes, it is."

Well, I didn't feel the need to say anything else. I nodded and said, "Have a nice time," and stomped up here.

I shut my door and threw myself on the bed. It was as if all the blood in my body had rushed up to my head. I wanted to open the door and slam it again, so hard that it came off its hinges and the whole house rocked.

I should be delighted. She isn't seeing Uncle Bert. She is seeing John Leakey. I have arranged it all. But I'm not delighted. I feel sick and . . . and . . . and what? I feel sick and jealous. There. I've said it. I know what the problem has been all along. John Leakey belongs to me. I want him for myself. I am in love with John Leakey the pharmacist. Me. Not Mother. Me.

And there's nothing I can do about it. Nothing at all.

Chapter Twenty-three

SATURDAY, MARCH 15
Bedroom, 8 p.m.

I dreaded going to work today. I thought he would be able to read my face. I didn't know how I would get through it.

When I got there, Gail greeted me by saying she'd heard I was a "proper little cook," which I suppose is better than "proper little madam," which is what I thought she was going to say. All day she got on my nerves, twittering like a sparrow. John came in late. I couldn't look at him. But he was in an efficient mood anyway, and just said, "Thanks for supper," before getting all beetle-browed over the prescriptions. Maybe he's embarrassed too. I love the way his hair falls over his face.

At about 11 a.m. Gail said, "Oh, look, there he goes again, your young man, up and down, checking that you're behaving yourself," and I looked up just in time to catch the tail end of William's bike flashing past the window. I rushed out and yelled down the street at him, so he had to brake and come back.

"What are you playing at?" I shrieked.

"I've got a new wheel," he said, all innocent. "Picked it up just now."

"Yes, but you're checking up on me. I know you are."

"I'm allowed to pass the shop, aren't I?"

"Gail says you're always passing." I had my hands on my hips. I felt like a fishwife, but even as I was yelling at him, I noticed the dark marks under his eyes, the white pinched look to his cheeks, and I felt a pang in my chest. He had that pathetic cornered expression on his face, like a sheep about to be sheared or a dog being whipped for someone else's crimes.

"Well, just don't," I said, and stalked back into the shop.

It wasn't until after lunch that John said anything to me. One of those lulls descended—there must have been a big soccer match on television or something—and Gail had taken the opportunity to pop out to Sainsbury's. He was doing some paperwork and I was standing by the register, twirling my foot.

He looked up and called over, "It was so nice of you to invite me on Wednesday. I had such a nice evening. I was really touched, Constance."

"Good," I said.

"And what a break from bacon sandwiches. Will I ever be able to go back to them now?"

He was trying to make me laugh. Had he guessed how I was feeling? "Humph," I managed.

"And your mother is so nice. Not at all how I imagined, I mean. . . ."

"What?" I said.

"Well, you're more like sisters, aren't you?"

Normally I enjoy the thought that we're like sisters—it makes me feel unconventional and romantic—but at that moment I wished she was pouchier and older, with gray hair at her temples, like Julie's mom. He was saying something else.

"Sorry?" I said.

"I asked about your dad. Do you mind me asking? When did he die?"

"Didn't she tell you? When I was a baby. He was in a motorbike accident. Delivering pizzas."

Most people grin when I tell them and they have to work hard to look serious. His mouth didn't betray the smallest of smiles. "How awful. And how hard for your mother."

"Yes."

"And it didn't work out with Cyril and Marie's father?"

"No. He kept having affairs." I wished he wasn't using me to find out this. Maybe he already knew the answers and just wanted an excuse to talk about her. Or maybe he was getting the practicalities over, leaving time for the two of them to discuss the meaning of the world, or *ER*, or whatever it was they've talked about so far.

"Well, she's amazing considering the life she's had. So funny and poised."

"Yes." My voice sounded odd to my own ears.

He was asking me more questions. When did she leave Paris? Would she ever go back? Until finally I said, "Why don't you ask her herself?" and it may have come out more crossly than I intended because he drew his chin in, said, "Okay," rather quietly, and went back to his prescriptions. I wished I hadn't offended him. I just couldn't stop myself.

Mother is out again tonight. She seemed a bit sheepish. Jack couldn't babysit because he's having a big bust-up with Dawn. After he'd called to tell her that, Mother said, "Babies, do you mind me popping out for a tiny while?"

Marie and Cyril were too involved in *Scooby Doo* to answer, but I said, "No. It's fine."

"I could cancel. . . ."

"No. Go."

"It's just . . . Constance . . ." There was a pleading expression in her eyes.

"Yes?"

"Things have been a bit crazy recently. I've been a bit involved, a bit all over the place, but this time . . . it's different. I feel more positive and, er . . . I want us to be a family."

"'S'all right," I said. She didn't move, just studied me. Shortly after that, she left.

I had one last brainwave, which has turned to nothing. Victor Savonaire is not, let's face it, a common name. I looked him up in the phone book and there he was. There was a moment of excitement and glory, but it came to nothing. When I rang, a woman answered. She called, "Vicki! Darling! Phone!" It must have been his fiancée. I could tell by the way she said his name. They must be back together, which explains why he didn't come to tea. I hung up before he came on the line. That's that, then.

William called around earlier, but I wouldn't let him in. I said, "I'm asleep," through the door, and after a little while there was a pile of chocolate on the mat and the sound of his footsteps retreating. Julie called too, but I told Cyril to say I was out.

The awful truth is that when you're unhappy, you're horrible to everyone and end up without any friends. And that makes you even unhappier. It's a vicious circle and I'm in the middle of it.

Chapter Twenty-four

Red roses on the doorstep this morning. And a note: "Do you believe in love at first sight? I do. J xx."

I wish I was dead.

Chapter Twenty-five

MONDAY, MARCH 17
School library, lunchtime

I've decided I can't work at the drugstore anymore. I realize this decision may sound sudden, but it is one I have been considering for some time. I don't want to let anyone down, but it's probably best if I leave straight away. I have greatly valued the experience I have gained in the post and will never forget the kindness and encouragement that has been proffered to me. I hope in the future I may even consider a career in the pharmacy business.

That's what I'm going to say anyway.

I can't, can't work there anymore. I just can't. Aghhghghg. It feels all murky and wrong. Wrong, wrong, wrong. It's too agonizing: the proximity to the man I love, the painful realization there is nothing I can do about it, that we're not talking boyfriend but *stepfather* material, that I'm too young for him ever to notice me anyway.

I shouldn't even think these things. It's wrong of me. Because Mother is a woman in love. She hasn't been out since Saturday, but she was on the phone giggling all yesterday evening. I should be happy for her. I don't deserve a Saturday job. I should go and work, for free, in an old people's home, or a hospital for very, very ill people, clearing out bedpans and listening to stories about the Second World War.

And that's another thing. *This* war. There are pictures in the papers every day of awful things. A bomb in a marketplace. In a cafe. Some women and children shot at a checkpoint. Soldiers everywhere. And I can't help thinking it's my fault. If only I was better behaved, and nicer, and more holy, and thought more about other people and less about stupid little me and my stupid little problems, maybe it wouldn't be happening. And when I think that, I also think, why doesn't God intervene to stop it? And the fact that he doesn't makes me wonder whether he exists at all.

Oh, it's all so messy.

I'm going to see John straight after school.

೫

The sitting room, 5 p.m.

I thought things were messy before? I didn't know the meaning of the word. What have I just done?

I left school with Julie and pushed my bike down the hill to her bus stop. She's lost interest in Mother and plans for my future stepfather. She doesn't even talk much about Uncle Bert. I've felt her enthusiasm in the project drift away since she met Ade. "I've never felt like this about anyone before," she said dreamily as we passed Prontaprint.

"Not even with Phil from college?"

"Especially not with Phil from college," she said. "Ade's different. He's—"

"More sophisticated," I said.

She rolled her eyes. "Yeah, he's that. But I forgive him. I don't know what it is. It's not just that he's gorgeous. He doesn't try and be cool or pretend he doesn't care. I've always found that really annoying before, but this time it's different. I don't know. He's got these melty brown eyes. When he looks at me, and we just stare at each other, I want to disappear into them. I get this feeling in my stomach. . . ."

"What kind of feeling?" I asked.

"Like I'm sort of collapsing, or it's all tightening up, almost like nerves, but much nicer. I can't really describe it. He makes me feel wrapped in a blanket and—"

"I think I know what you mean," I said.

I didn't wait for her bus like I sometimes do. I wanted to get it over with.

Gail was behind the counter. She was serving a woman with a tiny snuffly baby. "I can give you saline drops for the blocked nose," she said. "It might help her appetite. Oh, hello, Connie."

John's raven head was bowed over paperwork in the pharmacy behind her. He looked up when I came through and smiled at me with his mouth closed and the corners turning down, a sort of preoccupied-with-money smile. "Ah," he said absentmindedly, "hello."

"John. Have you got a moment? There's something I've got to talk to you about."

"Just a sec," he said, turning back to his books.

"It's important." I was biting the inside of my mouth so hard I thought I'd taste blood. If I didn't get it out quickly, I was going to cry.

He looked up again. He was wearing a soft wool sweater the color of the bay tree in our back garden, a green that's almost black. I wanted to bury my face in it. I thought it would smell of cucumber and herbs and Comfort. He didn't say anything, just moved his head very slightly in the direction of the chair beside him.

"Okay," he said gently after I'd sat down. We had our backs to the shop. His knees were under the desk; mine were at an angle to his. I remember staring at the fabric of my trousers, watching as the yellow flecks seemed to separate from the red ones, imagining them pulsing and moving. I heard the register beeping and the door opening and closing behind us.

I thought I had my speech planned, but it had gone. He said, "Is there something wrong at school?"

I shook my head.

"Or is it a . . . health thing?"

"No." I managed a smile. "No. It's . . ." And then it came out in a rush. "I can't work here anymore."

"Oh, Connie." He drew back slightly. "What a shame. Is it your exams?"

"Yes. No."

"What is it, then?"

I stared at the desk and tried to get back on track. "I realize this decision may sound sudden, but it is one I have been considering for some time."

"But you haven't been here some time yet. Is it something I've done or said? I know I can be a bit moody. Or is it that the job's boring? I'm just sorry to lose you, that's all. Not just your chicken à la mushroom, but your knowledge of tapeworm has been greatly beneficial."

I couldn't think of anything to say.

And then he put on an American accent and said, "I like having you around, kid."

I laughed, still staring ahead, and then stopped. The papers on the desk shuffled and swam. The wall, a medicinal pink, went pale and watery. And then I felt his touch on my chin, his fingers cool and soft and smelling of toast. He drew my face around so that he could look at me. "What's really the matter?" he said quietly. "Why are you crying?"

And then it was as if a catch that had been holding everything back broke loose and I threw my head at his shoulder, like a child head-butting its parent in a tantrum, and I heard myself whisper from the crook of neck and soft green wool that smelled, of course, not of cucumber and Comfort but bacon, "It's about you and Mother, which is great. But I . . . I . . . have this feeling in my stomach when I see you and . . . and . . . I'm in love with you myself."

Even from the center of the storm in my head, I felt him tense and his arms, which had responded to my collapse upon him by going around me, though they didn't loosen or drop, shifted slightly, so that his hands were holding my shoulder blades firmly in place, like brake pads. I knew then where I'd gone wrong; that any dream I had been carrying in my heart that I hadn't dared admit even to this book, even to myself, wasn't going to happen. He drew away, held my arms, and tried to look into my face. I didn't care then what he saw. It was all too late. He'd seen it already. I was beyond humiliation.

"Connie. You're very sweet. And I'm terribly touched. But I'm almost thirty. I'm far too old for you."

"But I'm grown-up for my age. People are always telling me that."

"Constance. You're sixteen! A couple of years younger, and you could be my daughter."

"But I'm not . . ." I stopped—how could I tell him my real age now?—and looked up at him and felt my eyes well with tears again.

"You need to fall in love with someone your own age."

"But everyone says how grown-up I am," I cried.

He smiled. "You're only sixteen," he said.

I wanted that thing Julie had been talking about, to be wrapped in a blanket and rocked. I wanted to curl up in a ball and for him to make it better. The room seemed to have gone dark. I managed to utter something about not telling Mother.

He said, "Sorry?"

"Don't tell Mother about this, please. Please don't, will you?"

He said, "Of course I won't, but"—he frowned—"but what did you mean? You said something about her and me being together. I don't understand."

"'S'all right," I mumbled. "I don't mind, really. I'm sorry I said it. It's just—" I had to stop or I was going to start blubbing again.

"She's a lovely woman and I really enjoyed supper the

other night, but I'm not going to ask her out, if that what's on your mind."

"But haven't you already?" I was already feeling foolish, but now I was beginning to get smaller, shrinking into my chair like Alice in Wonderland—becoming tiny and inconsequential, smaller than the smallest small thing.

"No!" He looked astonished.

"But haven't you been taking her out?"

"No!"

"And calling her?"

"No!"

"And leaving flowers?"

"NO!"

"Well, who has?" I said, confused. There was a box of tissues on the desk and I grabbed one and blew my nose.

"I don't know. But it's not me." I put the tissue up my sleeve and caught him making a gesture over my shoulder to Gail. The gesture involved his watch and me and a bit of a shake of his head. It was a gesture that said, "I just need a couple of minutes here," and I realized it was time to go. I had to find a stone to crawl under.

I stood up and muttered something about a misunderstanding. He said, "Please reconsider the job, Connie, though I do understand, of course, if you do think it would be difficult."

I tried to stand straight, and with as much dignity as I could muster I said that I really felt my decision should remain as it was, that maybe sometime in the future I might consider a career in the pharmacy business. The experience had been invaluable and . . . I stopped. "Sorry," I whispered.

He smiled at me and put his hand briefly on my shoulder. "All right," he said. He is kind and nice and gallant enough to put regret into that one word, but I know I saw relief in his eyes. I'd got everything wrong, I realized that now. I could feel the tears pricking again, so before he could say anything else, I pulled away and fled from the shop.

Outside the sky was thunderous. Black clouds were scudding across the gray, which was why it had become so dark inside. The rain was just beginning to fall, splattering a pattern on the pavement. In my confusion I grabbed my bike and, pushing it, ran left from the shop instead of right and found myself heading back up toward school rather than home. I stopped at the lights. My hair was flat against my scalp. The rain was hitting my shirt like bullets. I put my face up and watched the drops falling out of the sky. I couldn't tell where the rain ended and my tears began. I was stupid and naive and wrong. The streets were empty. I felt totally alone.

But I wasn't. Because there, wheeling up and down the pavement, was William.

He was on his bike, the wheels spraying arcs of water behind him. He must have been hanging about for some time. His hair was spangled with raindrops. His trouser legs were dark with damp and there was a wet streak up the back of his jeans.

"Have you been waiting for me?" I said.

"You don't have a coat."

"I know. Have you been waiting for me?"

He didn't answer. He'd got down from his bike and was taking his parka and putting it around my shoulders. "I saw you go in and thought you might not be long and we could bike together and then, when it started raining, I thought you might need this."

For a moment I felt like shrugging it off, but it was still warm from his body. It felt heavy and reassuring. The pockets hung down, with bits of junk and loose change. "My knight in shining armor," I said.

"More like your knight on shining aluminum."

I laughed, which made me choke, and before I knew it I was crying again. And this time I couldn't stop. It was raining properly now. And I just stood there sobbing, with William standing by me. He didn't put his arm around me. He just stood there, not awkwardly, just sort of waiting. After a bit he said, "Shall we go somewhere?"

and I nodded and followed him. He led us back to my house and took the key from me when I fumbled at the door. We went into the hall, both soaked to the skin. He leaned his bike against mine, removed his parka from my shoulders, laid it over the banister, pulled his own sodden sweater over his head, and went upstairs to get some towels. I went through into the sitting room and sat on the sofa.

I hadn't put the lights on and it was dark in there. I heard steps coming back down. William sat next to me. He leaned across me and switched on the side light. Then he handed me a piece of paper. He said, "Note on the stairs from the decorator." I read it through my wet eyelashes. It said, "Dear B, Gone to buy more paint. Call you later? J xx."

I'd seen the writing before. "Call you later?" "Do you believe in love at first sight?" It was the same handwriting. I'd seen it on that mystery valentine card, too—now I thought of it.

"J"? "J" for *John*. For *John Spence*.

I began to laugh hysterically. It wasn't John Leakey that Mother had been seeing, but John Spence. Our landlord, John Spence. With the pale knees and the "Wotcha, kids" and the Lycra shorts.

"It's John Spence," I said hysterically. "Mother's fallen in love with John Spence!"

William had brought a towel down and had been rubbing his head. He broke off and stared at me oddly. "You all right?"

"It hadn't crossed my mind. I mean, he's so awful!" I started laughing again. Then I noticed William's hair was sticking up like a hedgehog. "Your hair!" I said, laughing some more.

"Easy," he said in a quiet voice. He put the towel over me and, clumsily, started rubbing my hair dry too. The rhythm of it made my laughter come out in jerks, and before I knew it they'd turned into sobs again.

"There," he said, releasing me after a bit. "We don't want you to catch a cold." He ran the towel around my face, like someone drawing a circle. He was being so tender I wanted to melt. "Now. What?"

I murmured, "Nothing."

"So what were you crying for? Why were you standing out there in the rain like a tragedy queen, then?"

"I . . ."

"What?"

I didn't know what I felt about anything anymore. It took a long while for any words to come, but finally I managed to say, trying to make light of it, "I've been such a fool."

"Tell me, then."

And so I did. Falteringly at first, then in a rush, it all

came out. Everything I'd been bottling up and failing to face up to, all the muddle and confusion in my heart and my head. I told him about how Julie and I had match-made Mother. About how much power we'd unleashed; how we seemed to be able to do anything we turned our hand to, and how we had created this horrible thing. I told him about Uncle Bert and how wrong for Mother he'd been; how miserable it had made me, and how cross and possessive it had made Julie. I told him that was what we'd fallen out over, that when we'd made up she'd decided John the Pharmacist was the next on our list, and how we'd match-made Mother and him too and . . . And then I cried for a bit and when I'd wiped those tears away, I told him how jealous and left out I felt. "And then I thought . . ." I said. My stomach gripped. The sobs were going to start again.

"What?" He was looking at me so sweetly, so unper-turbed by my shocking disclosures, I felt I could tell him anything.

"That I was in love with him myself."

I caught him frown very slightly and then he looked away. I just thought he thought I was being stupid, a fourteen-year-old saying she was in love with a twenty-nine-year-old.

"What about your mother?" he said.

"That's what I mean." I picked up the note. "It was

John Spence, not John Leakey, all the time."

"Oh, I see," he said.

I should have told him then how I'd thrown myself at John; what a fool I'd made of myself. How I'd been wrong about that, too. But there was a funny expression on his face, like he thought I was stupid to have even imagined myself in love with someone so much older, like I was deluded. And I don't know what came over me then—a last flash of pride after an afternoon of humiliation—but I wanted to make him think that it *wasn't* that stupid, that it *was* possible. So I said, "So John Leakey's free, after all." I looked away.

So did William. "Right."

There was a long silence.

After a bit I said, "Shall we put the television on, then?"

He said, "I ought to be going."

Then I wished I *had* told him. I didn't want him to go. I wanted to feel close to him again. He didn't move, though, so in a small voice, I said, "Please don't go." I wanted him to stay really badly. The thing about William is he's so *comforting*.

His voice sounded strange, very distant. "Yeah. All right." He pressed a button on the remote control.

"Give me a hug," I said. I felt lonely. That's my only excuse. He shrugged his arm around the back of the sofa so that I could feel the dampness of his T-shirt across the nape of my neck. His fingers rested without pressure on my arm. I imagined them bridged, like someone throwing the shadow of a spider. The picture came to life on the television. Except it wasn't the television. It was the video. My father's tape was still in the machine.

"It's the Carrrrib-vod ad," I said.

I thought William would laugh and fiddle with the controls, but he didn't, and we watched my father frolic on the pier with his pretend friends and then jump, care-free, young, single, dead, into the Caribbean Sea. I put my head on William's shoulder, so my tears could run off my nose into his half-wet T-shirt. When the picture dissolved into gray fuzz, neither of us moved.

"Maybe . . ." he began after a while.

"What?"

"Connie, maybe the man at the drugstore is a father figure or something."

"Maybe," I said, not looking up. I wanted his hand to grip my arm, not just rest there. I moved my face farther into his chest. Under his top, it was bony and close, not firm and bulky like John Leakey's. I blotted my wet eyes against the fabric. I'd never noticed how delicious William smelled. It was like breathing in the wind from a bike, of fresh air and sweat, of pavements and chewing gum, and something sharp like soap.

He made a sort of noise above me and I did feel his fingers tighten. I knew what would happen if I raised my head but I raised it anyway and there was his face. I didn't notice anything about him but his eyes looking into my eyes. He said something, but I didn't hear it and I didn't answer because he'd moved his head down and kissed me.

It was so different from that time at the disco when the only thing I was aware of was the size of that boy's tongue. This was proper. I don't mean there were fireworks in my head. I didn't feel the world spin. I just felt the softness of his lips, so gentle, and then firmer, so that I felt his teeth through his lips and then his mouth began to open and I could feel things happening inside me that I'd never felt before. My hands were deep in the dampness of his hair.

And then the television blared on. The video must have got to the end of the tape and the screen reverted to *Newsround*—with the volume up too high. We both jumped and laughed. William reached for the control and switched the sound off. Then he looked at me. He gave a sort of sheepish smile. He had swiveled his body so that he was lying farther back into the cushions, and his legs were up on the sofa now.

"Oh," he said. His eyes were half closed. His face came closer toward me again. On it was the expression on his face that I think of as goofy. William's goofy expression.

William's goofy about-to-snog-me expression.

I leaped up. "William!" I said. "You're my friend. We're friends. Stop it. Don't look at me like that. Get up."

"What?" he said, looking dazed. "What do you mean?"

I was waving my arms around, shaking my head. "Don't. Don't look at me like that."

"Like what?"

"Like . . . like . . ."

He put his hand out and tried to pull me down. "Come here," he said.

I yanked away. "No. William. We mustn't do this."

"Do what?"

"We mustn't kiss each other."

"But I want to kiss you. I've wanted to kiss you for ages."

"Well, you can't," I said.

His sleepy expression had begun to harden into something more resentful. He sat up. "Didn't you like it?"

"What?"

"That. Just then. Me kissing you."

"No. Yes. No. I don't know." All I felt was confusion and fear. Granny Enid's always saying men take advantage of Mother. I said, "I was taking advantage of you. I liked it but I shouldn't have. You're my friend. I know you, you . . . you like me. I don't want to lead you on."

"What do you mean?" He was looking sullen now.

"If you kiss me, you'll want to go out with me. I don't want to go out with you."

"What, never?"

"I don't know. I'm not like Delilah. I don't want to try things out. I want to wait for The One."

"Right." His voice sounded louder than usual and more uncouth.

"I'm sorry," I said.

"I'm off, then."

He got up and went into the hall. I didn't follow him. I know it sounds awful, but I wanted him to leave. I heard the clank of the change in his parka pocket and the scrape of his bike, a muttered oath, and the rattle of the door, the rush of the rain on the sidewalk, a passing car, and then a slam and he was gone.

I sank back into the cushions, in the dark sitting room. Maybe I'd have cried if I'd had any water in my tear ducts. I felt hollowed out and distant from myself, as if all the events of the afternoon, all the revelations, the humiliations and the snogging had happened to someone else. I was too confused to think about John Leakey. I didn't want to think about William. Or even Mr. Spence. I just wanted to be alone. And that's where I am still, sitting on the sofa in the dark, more miserable and confused than I've ever been in my life.

Chapter Twenty-six

*W*illiam didn't call for me this morning. I didn't think he was going to, but I waited just in case. It was assembly, so I ended up being late. I had to sit next to the teachers. William was at the end of a row quite near me, but he didn't turn in my direction. His face looked rigid.

He ignored me at break and he ignored me at lunch. He even ignored me after general studies when Chloe stopped me halfway out of the classroom to say, "Got your euros for France yet, Connie?" And he walked right between us as I was reminding her I wasn't going.

I suppose I understand. I led him on, didn't I? It was a moment of madness. And it *was* nice. But I mustn't think about it. I mustn't. In the dark hours of last night I wondered whether I'm afraid of . . . I can't even say it . . . of sex. What if it's awful, or I'm awful at it? I'd rather try it out with a stranger, not someone I know well, not William. It's embarrassing for one thing. And he can't be The One. I know him too well. I know all his faults and his stupidness—his crap French accent and the way he narrows his brows and tries to look cool when he's feeling miserable. Julie says she loves Ade because he doesn't try to hide how much he likes her, but it doesn't work for me. If William liked me less, I might like him more.

I've tried to talk to Julie. We sat on our bench at break today. It was warm sitting there; the sun was on our backs. You could hear birdsong. I didn't mention what a fool I'd made of myself with John Leakey. I have to keep that to myself forever and ever, but I brought her up to speed on Mr. Spence. "Oh," she said, putting about fourteen scandalized syllables into that one word. I was encouraged by that. I began to express my horror and disgust—I think I mentioned his satin shorts—but she laughed, picked at a splinter of loose wood on the bench, and said, "Mission accomplished." So I knew she wasn't going to help me change the situation. It seems Uncle Bert is taking her and Ade to the Hard Rock Cafe for lunch on Sunday. "Sue will probably come along too," she said.

I remembered Sue punching the sports bag and felt glad. I said, "Are they back together?"

I thought Julie might be upset, but she smiled and said, "Yeah. 'Parently. He picked her up from the airport when she got back from Australia. Still, I've got her trained now. She knows not to mess with me." She was using the splinter of loose wood to carve a heart in the back of the bench. I suppose her mind's on other things.

"William kissed me yesterday," I said.

She dropped the wood. "No! You strumpet! You piece of work! Well?"

I told her the story, concentrating on the rain and cutting out the tears (and the reason for them).

"Was he good?" she said.

"I don't know. Julie! How can you ask that? How would I know? It was quite nice. But then he—"

"What?"

"He got this expression on his face, sort of lovesick."

"Oh." She smiled knowingly. She said a few things about "the balance of power" in relationships, but the subject led pretty swiftly back to Ade. The Perfect Boyfriend. The Love of Her Life. The One. They're going together to Delilah's party on Saturday. I said, knowing that she doesn't really like Delilah, I thought she'd have better things to do. She said it would be a laugh. And, anyway, before the party, in the afternoon, she and Ade are going shopping together, and after it they're going to go back to her dad's—who, though Julie's mom doesn't know it, is away on business. And, with the flat to themselves, "I think we might . . . you know—" She winced, tensing her shoulders at the same time.

"What?"

"You know."

"What?"

"Do it."

"Really?"

"Yes!"

People can really surprise you. I thought Julie had slept with loads of boys—well, at least Phil from college.

I said, trying to sound cool, "Haven't you already?"

"No! Not with . . . not with anyone! It's not that I've been saving myself. It's more that . . . I haven't really wanted to?" She put this like a question.

I said I understood. Maybe I'm not so far behind all my friends as I think.

"Don't tell anyone, will you?" she said, suddenly squeezing my hand. I wasn't sure if she meant I wasn't to tell anyone that she was going to sleep with Ade, or that I wasn't to tell anyone that sleeping with him would be her first time, but I nodded and shook my head to cover both possibilities. "Cross my heart," I said. The bell went then, and as we got up I gave her a quick hug for luck.

This afternoon on the way home I crossed the road when I got to the drugstore. When I got in, I watched the news. They had some politicians on talking about a peace process. Before I could stop myself I thought, "Oh, I can't wait to talk about that with John," but then I remembered. Today, even from the opposite sidewalk, I could see a new patch of white in the window—a notice about another antiwar march, or notification of a staff vacancy?

Tanya and Marcus, Delilah's parents, were packing up their car as I turned into our street. They're off for a day and night's sailing first thing tomorrow. Marcus had a squishy blue bag decorated with a pristine white anchor over his shoulder. He was wearing pink trousers and Docksiders: proper boating gear. "Sure we can't tempt you this time?" he said when he saw me. I know he was only trying to be friendly, but it's very annoying when people—usually adults—pretend they've asked you something, or invited you somewhere, when they haven't. I thought of answering, "Oh, okay, actually I'll come," to see what he said. Instead I grinned stupidly and said, "I'll let you know when my sea legs arrive."

"You do that," he said. "And perhaps you could get some for Delilah while you're about it."

We all laughed, but I could see Tanya glance anxiously back at the house. "Your mom says she'll keep an eye on her, and you'll pop in, won't you? She's got a lot of schoolwork, but I'm worried she might be lonely."

"Of course I will," I said.

Lonely! Delilah lonely! If only she knew.

I'm up in my room, with the window open. It's still light out. It'll be the Easter holidays soon. Everyone in the whole world is going to Paris on the French exchange. Except me. I'll be stuck here. I'll have to bury myself in work. Enough of love, the Library Crew beckons.

I miss William. I thought he might drop off some chocolate, but he hasn't.

Mr. Spence is finishing off the tiling. A little while ago he called up, "Fancy a cup of Rosie Lee?" And even though I want one, I told him he could piss right off with his Rosie Lee. Actually I said, "I'm fine, thanks." What does Mother see in him? And what shall I do about it?

Chapter Twenty-seven

SATURDAY, MARCH 22 *(or rather,
very early on* SUNDAY, MARCH 23)
My bedroom floor, 4 a.m.

A dispassionate account of the worst day of my life.
(Yes, even worse than Monday.)

Mother wanted to know why I wasn't at the drugstore. I told her Mr. Leakey didn't really need me anymore and how, what with SATs coming up, I felt it best
to concentrate on my studies. She accepted this without
comment. In fact, there was a little flicker on her face
that I read as a dawning suspicion that maybe some
mothers might have insisted I give the job up anyway.

She said, "So, are you going to study now?"

I said I was and, when they were all dressed, she took
Cyril and Marie off swimming.

Peace. But then I started missing William and feeling
bored. I can't remember what I used to do on Saturdays
before the drugstore.

I went around to Delilah's.

It had been playing on my mind that today was the day of the party. I wondered how prepared she was, mentally and physically, for the ordeal that was about to befall her. It was like knowing an accident was going to happen, a terrible pileup on the motorway, and being powerless to do anything to stop it.

She and her friend Sam were sitting wrapped in towels at the kitchen table doing their toenails. Sam's were candy pink, Delilah's licorice black. They had cotton balls between their toes, and on top of the varnish they were placing nail stickers in the shapes of hearts and flowers. The sink was piled with plates. They'd only been on their own a few hours and they already seemed to have got through most of the dishes. On the table was the remains of their breakfast: a carton of orange juice and a tub of Ben & Jerry's Chunky Monkey.

I asked if they were ready for the evening. Delilah rolled her eyes and said no, they had so much to do. "I mean, we've done our nails, but we've got our legs and underarms, and our tans to put on. I don't know what to wear yet. I'm either going to go kind of punk-rock-chick glamour, with that new drop-waisted skirt I've got. You know, with the pink trim? Or I'm going to really downplay and wear jeans with my fishnet stockings and those silver sandals? Sam's thinking the same, aren't you, Sam?"

"Yeah."

"What are you going to wear, Connie? Wellies or those burgundy peep-toe sandals." She and Sam giggled.

"Ha. Ha," I said. "Very funny."

"We're going to set up the bathroom like a spa. I've got all Mom's Clarins moisturizing stuff lined up ready. And our hair . . . I'm thinking little bunches. And we're going to do our makeup really properly, you know, take time over it?"

"I see." I looked up the steps into the back sitting room, at all the blond wood and white upholstery and freshly plumped cushions. "Do you want me to help clear some furniture?"

Delilah made a vague gesture with her hand. "Do you think we need to?"

I tried to keep the anguish out of my voice. "Yes."

"It's all right. Sam and I will do it later. I thought we'd close the double doors between the two sitting rooms and have music and dancing in the back room, with the stairs down to the kitchen, where the drinks will be, and move the sofas and chairs into the other, where we can turn the lights down really low for anyone who wants"—she and Sam giggled—"a bit of time out."

"And have you bought the booze?"

"Yeah," she said vaguely again. "Sorted."

"And the music . . . ?"

"My brother's doing it," explained Sam. "He's only twelve, but he really knows his stuff and he's got an iPod."

"That's all right, then," I said.

"And Will's on the door. If you see him, will you remind him?"

"I will if I do," I said, knowing I wouldn't. "So I'll be around at what time?"

Delilah mock-panicked, making startled eyes at the clock. "The invitation said eight p.m., so anytime about then. Or drop around later if you like."

"What about the carpets?" I said. "Shall we try and cover them?"

Delilah looked hassled. "Don't nag. There's shampoo under the sink if we need it."

I left. I'd done my best.

When I got back into our house, the rest of the day *dragged*. I was so bored I felt like throwing myself out of the window just to see something happen. Messy, but at least *interesting*. I couldn't call Julie because she was with Ade. I couldn't call on William because he hated me. I couldn't go to the high street in case I saw John. And I couldn't go anywhere near Delilah because of the "spa." I know what a spa within twenty paces of Delilah means: orange-and-oatmeal face packs.

I mooched. I tried on clothes. I got cross with Marie for playing her recorder too loud. I buried my face in the cat's fur and then kicked him off the bed for dribbling. I sat on the roof and listened to the traffic, snailing, snarled, circling the suburbs forever. I changed my mind and went downstairs to go to Delilah's. Changed my mind again and went to the fridge. I ate a rice cake. And then another. I watched the news. I told Mother that she looked lovely, and made a face behind her back. I hugged Jack. He was on his own for once, having split up with Dawn. (Dawn has finally broken.) And then I said, "Get off," and went back upstairs. And at eight o'clock, finally, I dressed (pink ra-ra skirt, denim jacket, red boots), said good night, promised not to be late, laughed at Jack's "call me if you need a lift home" jokes, and left for the party.

Delilah opened the door. Her face fell when she saw me. "No one's here," she squealed. "I can't bear it. It's all a failure. I'm a social disaster. I wish I was dead."

She had obviously opted for rock-chick. She was wearing a black halter-neck top, decorated with a diamanté heart, which showed off her soft golden shoulders, and a black skirt with a jagged hem, which hid her curvaceous tummy. On her legs were large-scale fishnets (the sort of net you'd need to catch a shark in rather than a sardine) and a pair of black biker boots with buckles. She had heavy kohl around her eyes and shiny crimson lip gloss that made her mouth look enormous. Delicate diamond pendants glinted from her ears.

"You look amazing," I said.

"Do you like my earrings?" she hissed. "They're real diamonds. They're Mom's."

We went into the front half of the sitting room, where the light was dimmed and music was playing. It was empty of furniture except for a couple of chairs, with girls on them, and a side table in the window, behind which crouched a small kid with two gold pendants around his neck (one in the style of a cross), voluminous jogging pants, and a cap at an angle. He was standing, fiddling with an iPod in one hand and making flicking hand movements—fingers stuck together in twos—with the other. He looked about ten except that he had a bumfluff moustache.

"That's Sam's brother," Delilah told me. "He wants to be a DJ . . ."

" . . . When he grows up," I said.

"Ssh." She gave me a look. "He comes with an iPod, so shut it."

"How can he afford an iPod at his age?"

"He has two buses and a train to get to school. His parents feel sorry for him. Also, according to Sam, they're so relieved to find he's got an *interest*."

I laughed, though Delilah didn't, and lifted my hand in the direction of Sam, who was sitting on one of the chairs, her fingers tugging at the smallest denim miniskirt I'd ever seen. She looked like she was shivering under her tiny camisole. She sent me a weak smile back. Her face looked spottier than usual. I wondered if the orange-and-oatmeal face pack had given her a rash. Standing next to her were two girls in bomber jackets and hoop earrings who were laughing hysterically while banging their hips together self-consciously in—sort of—time to the music.

Delilah shouted at me to come and get a drink. I followed her to the kitchen, where the table was laid out with plastic cups, a washing-up basin full of a mysterious dark-red potion, bobbing with bits of apple and orange, a few bottles of beer, some baguettes, and, touchingly, half a Brie.

"You've got the cheese in, then?" I said, trying to conceal a smile. Marcus and Tanya always provided half a Brie along with the Pimm's at their summer party.

"Soaks up the booze," she said. "We don't want people getting too drunk."

She ladled me a cup of the dark-red brew, which I took a quick sip of. It tasted astringent, half smoky, half sweet, with a vicious undercurrent that caught the throat. I coughed. "God. What's in it?"

Delilah giggled. I caught her glance toward a black

garbage sack in the corner, with some bottles sticking out. "Don't ask," she said. "Sam and I have been experimenting. Call it the Delilah Bite."

I took another sip. "Ow."

She laughed. Then the doorbell went and she scampered off to answer it. There was a burst of giggles. I could see down the hall that another gaggle of girls had arrived, all with side partings and long blond hair that looked like it had been ironed. Delilah brought them down to the kitchen, where they poured cups of punch and giggled some more. I realized there were about fifteen girls here now, to one prepubescent boy. Perhaps I'd been wrong to worry. Perhaps this was as bad as it was going to get. Then the doorbell went again. Delilah squawked and disappeared. This time I followed her up and reached the hall as she opened the door to William.

He seemed taken aback by Delilah's appearance. He'd been leaning against the doorframe, with that I'm-too-cool-for-this-life expression he sometimes gets, and I'm sure he swayed in shock. "Hi," he said, staring at her, as if that was all he could manage.

She giggled. "You might have smartened up for me a bit, Will." He was wearing several faded T-shirts in layers, an inside-out hooded top, and his Adidas sneakers. "Is that bike oil on your jeans?"

He bent down to look and she tapped his nose on the

way up. "Made you look, made you stare, made you lose your underwear!" (We'd all notice if that happened. His underpants were sticking out of his trousers, as usual.)

He crooked his arm around her neck, twisting her around and pretending to strangle her.

"Help!" she cried. "Con."

He couldn't pretend I wasn't there anymore. He dropped his arm. "Hi, Connie," he said, not looking at me.

"Hi," I said, looking away too.

I think she took him down to the kitchen then to "meet some of the girls," but I went the other way into the wide-open space of the sitting room, where I watched the joined-at-the-hip disco divas lark around, and made desultory conversation with Sam. She told me she was in love with Charlie from Busted, that he was a dark, deep soul stuck in a business that didn't understand him. Her brother came over and, in a voice that kept jumping between treble and base, said Charlie from Busted had no true musical integrity and wouldn't last. And she said what did he know, he didn't understand, he didn't recognize true talent when he saw it. "Twerp," she added as he headed back to his iPod.

I can't remember much more about the early part of the evening, except that it was cold—Delilah opened the back door when people started smoking—and that I wandered back and forth between the kitchen and the sitting room, avoiding William and trying to look as if I was having a nice time. A few more people arrived—a couple of lads in dark-blue jeans and zip-up sweaters from the youth club, more girls in various states of undress from the high school. One of the boys in a zip-up sweater tried to make conversation with me. Turns out he wasn't from the youth club but had met Delilah when she was on holiday in the Isle of Wight. His name was Cal. He asked me questions about school and Delilah. He said, "Constance is a lovely name." I told him it was French and that I loved France. He said he did too. French bread. French cheese. I was quite enjoying myself until he added, "French kissing." I was so embarrassed I had to walk off.

William took up position on the door at about 9 p.m. I don't know what his brief was. It's not as if there was a guest list or anything. I think it just made him feel important.

It got louder—a couple of drinks got spilled, someone went upstairs and unraveled a toilet paper roll on the banisters. Someone else, in search of attention, got locked in the bathroom. There was a huddle in the "quiet" (i.e. snogging) room and a waft of smoke in the doorway. A cigarette was stubbed out on the kitchen floor. But these were all isolated incidents, identifiable, controlled. The cigarette burn was small and close to the sink. So when

Delilah came up to me when I was in the kitchen picking at the Brie and yelled, "Ashtrays! Have you got any ashtrays next door? There's ash being dropped all over the floor!" I didn't panic unduly. I felt we'd encompassed the worst. That Delilah, as usual, had got away with it. No gatecrashers. No mass descent. And I said I'd go and get some, relieved to escape from my own social embarrassment, to give my face a break from its false, I'm-quite-happy-on-my-own smile.

"Leaving already?" said William harshly as I sidled out. I didn't even answer.

Back at home Cyril had gone to bed and Marie was asleep with her head on Jack's lap. He was watching some detective drama. Or trying to. You could hear the bass line of next-door's music through the walls, along with the noise of people in the street.

Jack raised his eyebrows when he saw me. "Home already, Cinders?" he said.

I gave him a hug, being careful not to disturb Marie, and told him I'd come to get a couple of ashtrays. He said I looked flushed. I was probably just still angry with William. But I said, so he wouldn't worry, "Too much dancing!"

"By the way, your mom out anywhere nice?" he said.

Normally, as you know, I tell him to mind his own beeswax, but an idea struck me then, out of the blue.

Jack may not be perfect, but he loves Mother, that's obvious, and at least he doesn't go jogging in satin shorts. From the start I've been determined that she shouldn't end up with him—I told Julie so, didn't I?—but desperate times mean desperate measures.

"No," I said. "She's out with our creepy landlord. You know, that weedy Mr. Spence? She needs saving, Jack. . . ."

And, leaving that thought with him, I collected the two ashtrays I could find and went back to Delilah's.

I'd only been gone ten minutes, but something had changed. William was being barged at the door by a group of boys in fur-lined parkas. A girl with scraped-back hair and hoop earrings was screeching in the middle of them, "We're invited! I've got an invitation." She thrust something under his nose and after that they burst past him, like water surging through a dam. I followed.

There were more bodies in the house. The hall was full. A picture had fallen off the wall and was on the floor, leaning against the baseboard with the glass across it cracked. Someone had been sick on the carpet on the stairs; a bunch of toilet paper roll had been stuffed on to the mess, but you could smell it. Shoes had stamped tread-shaped puke stains all the way up to the landing. The front room was heaving—people were dancing and jostling. I saw Joseph Milton right in the middle of them. The music was very, very loud. It wasn't coming from Sam's brother's iPod—both Sam's brother and the iPod had vanished—but from a large portable stereo, pumping out bass. I was holding the two pathetic ashtrays in my hands, so I put them on the mantelpiece. It was like arriving with a couple of life belts half an hour after the *Titanic*'s gone down. Ash, spilled beer cans, splattered Delilah Bite everywhere.

In the kitchen I found Sam leaning into the sink.

"You all right?" I yelled to get her attention. When she turned her face to me it was bleary, her mouth spittled. She made a sound and then retched. I pushed past the girls shrieking at each other behind her, and reached her just as she vomited. "Okay, okay," I said, pulling her hair back. "There you go. Oh. Gosh. There you go."

"Ughghhh," she said.

There was still washing up in the sink—a couple of mugs and plates—so I had to retrieve them before getting the sick down the drain. I used the wrong end of the washing-up brush. It was mainly Delilah Bite, with bits of apple in it. It could have been worse.

I went upstairs to see if I could get some towels from the bathroom, but even after I'd scrambled over the group on the floor, I found I couldn't get in. The door was locked. Suspicious "sounds" emanated from inside.

Okay. Back through the legs. Back downstairs. When I reached the kitchen, Sam was leaning against the sink, facing out now, which was a good sign. Her face was very pale. "Have you got a coat?" I said.

She managed to tell me she had a jacket under the stairs, which I found and struggled her into. Then I led her into the garden and put her on the wooden recliner—what Marcus calls his "steamer chair"—for some fresh air while I got help.

"Delilah?" I said. "Do you know where she is?"

Sam's head was lolling. Her eyes were half closed. "Quiet room," she mumbled.

Of course.

I wended my way back through the kitchen, to the section of the house dedicated to those who wanted "a bit of time out." The door was ajar and I pushed it open. At first I couldn't see anything. The only light was the strip showing under the double doors to the front room. My eyes got accustomed to the dark. All the furniture in the house seemed to be in here, and on each piece, and on the floor in between, there were entangled couples.

"Delilah!" I hissed. "Are you in here?" Nobody stirred. "Delilah!" I put more urgency into my voice. No reaction. "Delilah! Sam is dying. Can you come and help?"

At this, the couple in the far corner, beyond the sofa,

came apart and Delilah emerged. She trod her way over. Her hair was disheveled, her eyes sleepy. The strap of her bra was hanging out of her top. "What you want?" she slurred, frowning. I wondered how many Delilah Bites she'd had since I last saw her.

As I explained about Sam, a bloke in a checked short-sleeved shirt followed her across the room, sidled past me through the door, and disappeared. "Dan!" she called after him. "Daa-mn." She swayed as she swore and, though the word began with feeling, it sort of tapered out.

"Not Dan Curtis again?" I said.

She blew out like a horse. "Damn," she said again. Then, "Oooh, look, Darius! DARIUS!" A guy in a skull-cap was leaning, one foot against the wall in the hall. I swear she said, "Cooeee." A lazy sort of grin crossed his face and he raised his hand and nodded a greeting at her.

"Anyway, she's in the garden," I said. "How am I going to get her back to East Sheen? Where's her brother?"

But it was hopeless. Delilah had hooked her bra strap back up and tottered off toward the bloke in the skullcap.

I stood looking after her for a moment. She had got there without falling over and was gesticulating and giggling up at him, circling her fingers across her bare shoulder, rotating her head to the music, swinging her hair. He leaned back, immobile, watching her. Then, a sleeping cobra striking, I saw him grab her head and kiss her on the lips, one of his hands continuing to hold her by the head, the other dangling casually by his side.

I would have walked away then, but there was a small agitation at the door beyond them. William was trying to greet some people, but they'd pushed past him. He looked up after them, and for a second our eyes met over Delilah and the boy in the skullcap—and I saw the anguish in his expression—before I realized that the couple stalking in were Julie and Ade.

She came straight up when she saw me. "Connie!" she said, and I could hear panic and misery. She wasn't even dressed in Julie party gear. No combats or string vests or dog-collar bracelets. No glitter or wild hairdo. Just jeans, her toweling hoody, and Alison's leather jacket. She'd done her makeup in a rush too, and there were clogs of mascara under her eyes. Her mouth was in a grim line. She looked like she was trying hard not to cry. She glanced over her shoulder. Ade had gone into the front room. "Connie," she said again.

I put my arm around her and pulled her into the kitchen. She was gripping on to my hand. "What's wrong?" I said.

She looked over her shoulder again. "Not here." She gestured urgently to the back door. "Out there."

Well, the steamer was taken—Sam had lolled completely to one side and it looked like she was asleep—but there was no one in the alfresco dining area. We sat on two of the chairs. You could look up at the house with all the lights on and music blaring; people moving across the windows. Julie crossed her arms on the table and buried her head in them. "Oh God, oh God."

"Are you okay?" I said. "Are you hurt or something? Is it Ade?"

"Yes."

"What happened?"

And then it all came out. How they'd met in the high street at lunchtime and had a fab couple of hours browsing. How they'd had a mocha and shared a sunburst muffin in Starbuck's, and that had been great. How she'd wanted to go to the cinema, but he'd wanted to go back to her dad's flat, but she'd persuaded him and how that had been cosy and snuggly, and how when the film had finished he'd said, "Can we go there now?" And she'd agreed, thinking she'd make him some food and they could have a snog and a cuddle and get ready for the party, *after* which, they'd go back for the Big Moment. But then when they'd got to the flat . . . She broke off and lit a cigarette, her hands fumbling at the package.

"Did you have a row?" I said.

"No. Yes. Sort of."

"What, then?"

"Well . . . as soon as we got through the door we

started kissing and it was lovely and we were on the sofa and it was all fine, but then he started getting more insistent and doing things, you know, under my top and stuff. That was okay, but then he started pulling off my trousers and I said, "No, let's wait." I wasn't ready, do you know what I mean? Maybe I was nervous. I wanted it to be later. Nighttime. I dunno why. I just did. That was what I had in my head. But he kept carrying on and saying things like, "Let's do it now." And then when I said no and sat up, he stalked off to the bathroom. So then I went to talk to him and then he started up again, about how we should do it now and I'd said I was ready for it and why was I backing down? And I didn't know what to say, it had gone all wrong. I'd just wanted to wait until later. Do you understand? He said I'd gone all frigid on him, and I suppose I had."

"Poor you," I said.

"But that's not all. Because then he got all cool and put his jacket on and said he was going for a walk. And I didn't want him to go, not like that, so I said it was okay and that we could do it now if that was what he really wanted. So finally he took his jacket back off and we went into Alison and Dad's bedroom and got under the covers and it was weird because the bed smelled of them and I felt really shy. He must have got undressed, but I didn't look at him, and then he was next to me and kissing me and, you know, Connie, I didn't feel anything. Just cold and scared. And after a bit, with me not moving or anything, he turned away. And then we both got up and got dressed again in silence. And then we came here."

"Oh, Julie," I said. "Poor you. How horrible."

"I'm going to be a virgin forever."

"Aren't we all," I said.

She laughed then and put her head back on the table, but with her chin up, the hand with the cigarette held away. "What a mess. I thought he was The One. I thought it was going to be . . ."

"I know."

We sat there for a bit longer. I said a few things about how these things happen, and how if he'd really loved her he would have been more sensitive to her needs.

"I wonder what Ade's doing now?" she said after a while.

"Do you want to go and find him?"

"Not really."

She seemed better now that she'd told someone. She gave a comedy groan, which ended in a shiver.

"Shall we go back in?" I said.

"Yeah." She stubbed out her cigarette on the table and threw it into the daffodils.

Sam stirred and made a sort of whimpering noise in

her sleep. I had to do something about her. I had to begin to think about getting her home before she caught pneumonia. And then there was Delilah. Snogging her way around the party. And then William, manacled to the front door, in a rage. And the missing twelve-year-old and his iPod. I sighed. Little pockets of anxiety everywhere. And as usual Connie Pickles, the only one in control. Julie put her arm through mine. "Once more into the breach," I said as we entered the house.

Things seem to have exploded even further in there, like a can of Coke that's been shaken before it's opened. There was pogoing behind the Brie. You could see up the stairs that the doors between the front room and the "quiet" room had been opened and loads of boys were jumping on the sofas and across the chairs. The music was even louder. Julie saw someone she knew and her face cheered up. I left her in what could be described as "animated conversation," if you can be animated shouting at a thousand decibels.

In the hall there was a new development. Delilah wasn't involved in tongue relay anymore. She was sitting on the stairs, leaning on the wall, between two boys. The one standing was the bloke in the skullcap; the other, sitting just above her, was Ade. She was rocking her head and singing. Ade saw me and started stroking her leg, starting at her ankle. She closed her eyes and he continued.

The bloke in the skullcap was just watching.

It was disturbing—degrading—seeing her like that. I shouted out was she all right, and she smiled at me and said, "Yeah, yeah." Then I gave Ade a look that should have vaporized him on the spot. What a bastard. Julie was still in the kitchen. I had to get back to make sure she stayed there.

The front door was half open and William was sitting outside on the step, swigging from a can of beer and smoking a roll-up. I tutted loudly, "William! What if the neighbors saw?"

"You are the neighbors," he said, and gave a shout of laughter.

"Can you come and help? Sam—Delilah's friend—is in trouble. I've got to get her into bed or home or something. But I can't lift her. And I've got to keep Julie out of the hall. Please."

He carefully extinguished the end of his roll-up and put it in his pocket, then heaved himself to his feet. "Where do you want me?"

We sidled past the weird threesome on the stairs—Delilah and Ade (the *total* bastard) were kissing now; the bloke in the skullcap was still there, but looking bored—through the kitchen, where Julie was still safely chatting to her friend ('Stay there!" I said), and into the garden. I pointed to the comatose bundle that was Sam. William went over and poked her, trying, unsuccessfully, to wake her up.

"I'll have to carry her," he said, heaving her into his arms. She stirred. Her head lolled on to his shoulder. "Okay. Here we go. Upstairs, I think, don't you?"

Our little procession made it back into the kitchen, through the people in the hall—"Excuse me. Thank you. Sorry. Can you— There we go. Okay. Sorry. Thanks"— up the stairs to the first floor, along the landing, and then up to Delilah's bedroom in the attic. There were pots of makeup and powder all over her desk and items of clothing and shoes all over the floor. A hand mirror with "Delilah" written in three-dimensional paint on the back was balanced on the window frame. William shifted Sam's weight from his arms to his shoulders and managed to launch her over the bars of the platform bed on to the mattress beyond. I climbed the ladder and covered her with Delilah's duvet.

"There," I said, smoothing her hair from her face. "She should be okay now." But when I turned around, William had left the room.

I'd had enough then. I stood looking out of the window at the patchwork of dark gardens below. The house seemed to shake and thump. If it wasn't for Julie and

Delilah downstairs, I would have tried to climb out, shinny across the roof to my own ledge. What was happening at home? What was Jack thinking? He couldn't have fallen asleep with the racket through the walls. Was Mother back? She wouldn't stand for it, that's for sure. Would she be with Mr. Spence? What was I going to do about that? I looked at my face in Delilah's hand-painted mirror. I looked pale and sober. On impulse I picked up a tube of lip gloss and ran it over my lips. It tasted like cherry chewing gum (which is nothing like cherries, but quite delicious in its own way).

And then I went back downstairs.

I could tell something had happened the moment I rounded the landing. Shouts were coming from the sitting room, not wild exuberant shouting, but angry shouting. I stood at the top of the stairs. The music suddenly stopped and the shouts became more distinct. Julie's voice was in there, angry but controlled. So was Delilah's—tearful. And a girl's voice I didn't recognize shrieked, "You slut! You slut!"

I jumped down the stairs and reached the sitting room as Toyah Benton charged at Delilah. Delilah was clinging to the boy in the skullcap, who was trying to get away from her. Toyah Benton didn't know who to clobber: the boy in the skullcap—Darius, oh, *Darius, that Darius*—or Delilah. Her fists were going everywhere. "You . . .

I'm . . . get that . . . I'm gonna . . . you . . ."

Then William was there, pulling her off them. Delilah fell back and started whimpering on the sofa. Two of the girls with long blond hair sprang out of the crowd to comfort her. Toyah Benton was yelling at William now, but he was saying something to her and slowly she stopped and started crying. Three girls came around her too, whispering to her, occasionally shouting abuse—"Howcouldyoudothattoher?"—at Darius, who was just standing looking hopeless, scuffing his feet, by the door. Not cool, but dim. People began to drift away. Toyah Benton stalked out of the house. Darius followed. You got the feeling their evening had only just begun.

I glanced around for Julie. I was sure I'd heard her voice. But I couldn't see her. Ade had disappeared too. William was standing by the group on the sofa. I remember thinking how all that biking had filled him out. He saw me watching and came over. "She's such a little idiot," he said. "She doesn't know what she's doing. Someone's got to take her in order before she gets herself into serious trouble."

There was a note in his voice I hadn't heard before. Not about Delilah anyway. What would you call it? Concern? *Tenderness?* I gave him a long look. I thought about him kissing me. "It looks like you're *her* knight in shining aluminum," I said finally.

I don't know what he was going to say then—it was the first time either of us had made any reference to the other afternoon—and now I'll never know because at that moment there was a renewed squeal from the sofa. The long-blond girls were on their knees on the floor, rummaging around in the cushions, while between them Delilah, her hands to her ears, was sobbing. "Mommy's earring. It's gone."

"More help is needed!" I said. William looked at me as if trying to read something in my face.

"Connie?" he said.

"What?"

He looked at me for a moment longer. "Nothing." Then he turned away and went over to Delilah. She wailed, "Will," and hugged him. I didn't wait to see what happened next. I left the room and went to find Julie.

She wasn't in the hall, or on the stairs. She wasn't in the kitchen. I finally found her back in the garden, having a cigarette. Her makeup was smudged under her eyes, but she was calm. Ade, she told me, had left. She never wanted to see him again. "What . . . what happened?" I asked.

"He and that drunk Darius were, what do you call it, 'sharing' Delilah. Taking it in turns."

"She's out of her head," I said. "She's been drinking all day . . ."

"I know. I don't blame *her*. Although I do think she needs to seriously rethink her life. I just think how desperate would you have to be to do that? Ade, I mean. It's like he had to prove something. Now I've chucked him he's begging me, saying he was just trying to make me jealous, but I don't care what it was. It's just pathetic."

"Yes."

"What a terrible party."

"Yes."

"They always are."

"Are they?"

Julie laughed at my expression. "It's the pressure of having to enjoy yourself. These are the best years of our lives. People are always telling us that, aren't they? So if you are not having the best time ever, you think, what's wrong with me? I'm missing out. Everyone else is having a great time and I'm not. But you know, sometimes I think, well . . ."

"What?"

"That we've got the rest of our lives too."

We sat out there for a long time, talking about this and that, until we got too cold to sit out any longer. Julie's mom wasn't expecting her home—she thought she was at her dad's, remember—so I asked if she wanted to sleep over at mine. She said she did. We got up—my limbs felt stiff—and went back into the party to say good-bye.

It was quiet now. Most people had left. The kitchen floor stuck to our feet as we crossed. Bottles lay everywhere. Three girls and Cal from the Isle of Wight were eating bread at the table. A boy with three earrings in one lobe had passed out in the corner. Through the door to the back sitting room, you could see two people lying together on the sofa.

I should have walked on, but I didn't. They were asleep. I stood in the doorway and watched them. Her head was on his shoulder. His arms were around her. Julie was waiting for me by the front door. I had to go. But I couldn't tear myself away. I thought if I stood there a little longer, William would wake up and see me. He would shake Delilah off. He'd come over to me. I'd never noticed how long his eyelashes were before, or how muscular his arms. He made Delilah look very small.

He was my friend, my best friend. He smelled of pavements and peppermint. And he was with Delilah.

What had I done?

"Are you coming?" Julie was outside, calling me. "I'm cold. I want to go to bed."

I pulled my eyes away and followed her to the door and out to the street. We let ourselves into the house. There was no sign of Mother or Mr. Spence. Jack had pulled out the sofa bed and was under the duvet, asleep.

We made ourselves some toast and tea and came up

here to my room. I made up a bed with the spare pillow and eiderdown on the floor, and we talked for a while. I didn't tell her about seeing William with Delilah. Not at first. Instead we talked about parents and love, about Ade. Julie said he'd made a fool of her and then, her voice croaky with tiredness, said some things about her step-mother she'd never said to me before, how she liked her, but she just wished she was someone else's stepmother, how she never got her dad to herself. I told her about Mother and how guilty I felt about our "games." "I wish we hadn't split her up from Uncle Bert now," I said.

"Did we?" she said. "I thought Sue came back from her work trip and whipped him in. We didn't do anything."

"Yes, we did. I said things to put Mother off, and made Marie sick. And—oh, I don't think I ever asked. What did you do that very first day, the day of your first date with Ade, to make him cancel?"

"I didn't do anything."

"You must have done. Why else did he cancel?"

"It was the day Sue got back. She rang to tell him to pick her up from the airport."

"Really? So that wasn't us . . . ?"

"Apparently not."

Then I told her about making a fool of myself with John Leakey; how I just cringe when I remember it now,

I don't know what I was thinking. She said how I shouldn't beat myself up and "Great arse." And we started laughing then and couldn't stop. When we finally managed to control ourselves she said, "What happened with William in the end?"

I lay on the floor, looking up at the ceiling. "I really like him."

"He's got a great arse too." We both laughed, but for not so long that time.

Finally I said, "I think he's with Delilah now."

Julie yawned. "That won't last," she said.

And pretty soon after that she was silent and I realized she was asleep.

Chapter Twenty-eight

Bathroom, 6:30 p.m. (still not
feeling too good)

Woken first thing this morning by the smell of bacon wafting up the stairs.

Retched and went back to sleep.

Woken the second time by Mother calling me to get up for church.

Groaned and went back to sleep.

Finally woke to the sounds of Julie moving around my room, getting her clothes on. "Lunch with Uncle Bert," she whispered, crouching next to me. "Gotta go."

She tiptoed out and I thought I'd go back to sleep again, but I couldn't. The events of last night seeped into my head. All I could think about was William. William, William, William. William and Delilah.

Downstairs was quiet. I wondered if they were all at church. When had Mother come back last night? Was

Jack still there? Was William still next door?

My head felt as if someone had sliced the top off and replaced it with sawdust. If I left my eyes open for too long, they began to dry out. Someone had been at them in the night with sandpaper. I tried to remember, but I think I'd only had one cup of Delilah Bite. There had been a moment of dizziness early on in the evening, but after that: nothing. So why did I feel so terrible now? Lack of sleep? Or William?

Tea started to seem the only thing for it, and I got out of bed—or rather off the floor—and made it downstairs.

I wasn't alone, after all. Cyril and Marie were in the garden. And Jack and Mother were sitting at the table, drinking coffee. "Aha!" Mother said brightly when she saw me. "Good evening?"

"Is it evening already?" I said.

"I meant did you have a good evening?"

"Yeah," I said noncommittally, and went into the kitchen. I could just *feel* their raised eyebrows behind me. This wasn't me. Some alien teenager had invaded my body.

When the kettle had boiled I slumped into the chair next to Jack, nursing my mug. "Still here?" I said. Was he acting on my tip-off of the evening before?

"Shouldn't I be?" he said. Mother laughed.

"Oh God. Whatever," I said, and stomped upstairs.

I had a shower in our new Mr. Spenced bathroom and

felt a bit better. When I came out, Jack was waiting on the landing. "You all right?" he said. "You seem a bit . . ."

"'Sfine," I said.

"Okay. Well, I'm off then—" He turned to go.

"Jack—" I said.

"Yeah?"

"Did you sleep over?"

He laughed. "Yes, but she didn't. You're not the only one who spent a night on the tiles."

"Oh." That was disappointing. (And, if it meant she'd spent it with Mr. Spence, *disgusting*.) Still, it was early days. I called after him, "Remember what I said, though."

He was halfway down the stairs, but he came back up and ruffled my wet hair. He shook his head. "You just worry about yourself, little one," he said.

I got dressed and told Mother I was going next door. Cyril and Marie were at a friend's and she was lying on the sofa having "a nice quiet afternoon"—for which read hangover. *The World at One* was on the radio in the background. The newscaster said something about the end of the war being in sight. "We'll have a chicken tonight, okay?" Mother said. "A special chicken."

I'd put on some of her lipstick. I didn't know if William would still be at Delilah's. *That won't last.* Julie had said that, hadn't she? And Julie usually knew about these things. Maybe it had ended already. I couldn't believe Delilah really cared for him. He was just one of her games, part of her collection, another name for the Snog Log. So I wouldn't be hurting her, would I, if I let him know how I felt? I kept replaying every nice thing William had ever said to me. The valentine card I'd been so rude about. I *knew* he liked me, so why did I feel so nervous?

Delilah's house was . . . well, to say it was a mess would be putting it mildly. It looked and felt as if an army of Labradors had waded through a muddy pond, splashed through a candy factory, and then bounded in and shaken themselves on every surface. And then they'd tucked any valuables under their paws and legged it.

A halfhearted cleaning process was under way. Sam was in the hall, sweeping broken glass into a dustpan. "Hiya," she said when she saw me.

"You all right?" I said.

"Yeah." She looked pale but alive. She'd probably had more sleep than the rest of us put together.

The furniture was back in the front room, and the doors to the back room were closed. There was a boy scrubbing the carpet, but it wasn't William—it was the bloke from the Isle of Wight, the one who'd made the French-kissing comment. Cal, was it?

"You're supposed to do circles working in," I said. "The other way around you're just spreading the stain."

He looked up. "Oh, hello. Did you crash here too?"

"No. I live next door."

He stood up and looked at his watch. "I'd better be off soon. I think I'll call a cab."

I said it must be expensive getting a cab all the way to the Isle of Wight and he laughed and said, "I don't live on the Isle of Wight. I live in Hammersmith. I just go there on holiday."

"Oh, I see."

He was saying something else, but I was trying to work out if it was William's voice I could hear in the kitchen.

"Sorry?"

He said, "I'm sorry if I scared you off last night."

"You didn't." It wasn't William's voice. It was too high.

"But you have got very nice eyes."

I was about to run away; that's what the old Connie Pickles would have done. But something stopped me. Nice eyes! I have nice eyes! I grinned instead, a stupid grin, I'm sure, but he grinned back and—you know what?—it actually felt quite nice.

"Connie! Connie! Help!! You're here! Thank God!" Delilah, passing the door, had spotted me. "They'll be back in an hour. What am I going to do?"

I left Cal ringing for a cab and followed her back

down to the kitchen. William wasn't there, but Sam's brother was sitting at the kitchen table, looking miserable. At least he was alive. Delilah, rummaging around under the sink for a bucket, explained someone had nicked his iPod. "Yeah, and I know what they look like and everything, and I'm going to come to your school and get them," he squeaked.

"But you didn't have a chance to 'get them' last night?" I said.

"Nah. I went up to her parents' room to think about it and I . . . I fell asleep."

"I seem to be the only one who didn't get a bed around here!" sang Delilah happily.

The only evidence of William was in her face. She was having problems with the floor—the more water she applied, the stickier it seemed to get—but she wasn't getting cross or panicked. She was laughing and fooling about. She'd had a shower and her hair was pulled up into a towel-turban. She was wearing the pink gown from Oasis that William had used that time to mop up the tea. For a girl who'd snogged three boys, caused two breakups, and drunk a gallon of mixed spirits, not to mention destroyed her parents' house, she was looking remarkably cheerful.

I couldn't stand it. I said, "Did you find Tanya's earring?"

Her face fell. Her mouth twisted in anguish. "No. No. I reckon that cow who tried to hit me nicked it. William and I've looked everywhere. I thought I'd put this one back in her jewelry box and it'll be ages before she notices and maybe she'll think she lost it herself. William says—"

I interrupted. "And the picture in the hall?"

"Don't! And the bathroom lock's broken." She wrinkled her nose. "There's Durex all over the floor. And the Madagascan fertility symbol's disappeared."

"I'm off." The boy from the Isle of Wight/Hammersmith poked his head around the corner. "Thanks for the party, Delilah. And, er, see you again, I hope . . ." He paused.

" . . . Connie," I added for him.

"Yeah. Connie."

I should have left then too. I wanted to. I wanted to go around and find William. But I didn't. I don't know why. Guilt? Fear? That old Pickles sense of responsibility? Instead I rolled up my sleeves and helped out. If I was going to betray Delilah, the least I could do was clear up first. Two of the girls with ironed blond hair were vacuuming upstairs. Delilah went up to tidy her parents' room. I attacked the puke stain on the stair carpet, scrubbed out the sink, and opened all the windows to get rid of the smell. Then I heaved all the trash bags over my shoulder and took them down to the house at the end of the street where you never see anyone go in or out, and which has the trash cans out all week. I thought I might bump into William but I didn't.

When I got back, the house looked much more presentable. It stank of Mr. Muscle and it still looked *ruffled*, but at least Tanya and Marcus weren't going to pack Delilah off to a juvenile delinquents' detention center the moment they walked in the door.

It would take at least an hour to notice the missing Madagascan fertility symbol. And then they'd pack her off to a juvenile delinquents' detention center.

Her friends with the ironed hair went, leaving just me, Sam, and Sam's little brother sitting at the kitchen table. Delilah had got dressed and jumped down the stairs effusive with thanks, calling me her "honey" and her "bestest, bestest friend." She is very generous like that. She doesn't take people for granted. God, how I wished at that moment that she did. And then the doorbell rang. Delilah squealed and ran to the kitchen window to check her reflection. She rubbed her teeth and had a quick gargle in the sink.

"That'll be him," she spluttered. "Let him in, Con. Go on."

Behind me, I heard Sam say, "Who's 'him'?"—the only one of us who didn't know.

I opened the door. He was leaning against the wall, in the same trousers as the night before and a faded green T-shirt that made his eyes seem very blue. He didn't look surprised to see me, but gave a lopsided sheepish smile. "Wotcha," he said.

The blood rushed to my face and then rushed away again. I stared at him. I think I swallowed. There was so much I wanted to say.

But he walked past me and jumped the steps to the kitchen. I could hear Delilah chattering away, and his own voice, deep and calm, asking after Sam's brother's iPod, being nice like he always is, like I've always taken for granted.

When I got down there he was sitting in the chair I'd vacated, and Delilah was perched on his knee, with her arms around his neck. I stood with my back against the cold, hard sink and I said something cold and hard like, "Good timing on the clearing-up front."

Delilah said, "He helped. Only earlier, didn't you, Will?"

"You stayed the night, then?"

Delilah giggled. William said, "I sort of crashed. I've just been home for some sleep."

He put his hands on Delilah's waist and gently lifted her, so he could stand up. "I've gotta go. I'm meeting my brother."

Delilah took him to the door. When she came back, I was sitting down. I wish she'd stayed all girly, but she was calm. Her eyes were wide with happiness and hope. "I really, really like him," she said in a normal voice, no theatrics. "I think he likes me, don't you? It's different this time. Connie, you're my friend. Tell me truthfully, don't you think this time it might work out? Do you think he might be my boyfriend?"

I looked into her face and told her that I thought it might, and that he probably would.

"Cross your heart?" she said.

℘

Back in bathroom, 9 p.m.

I've had to take a break for a chicken dinner. We had a guest. A guest of honor. Mother got out the napkins. It wasn't a guilt supper, but an introductory supper. A meet-and-greet supper. You can guess, can't you? Mr. Spence. Or rather, *John*.

I tried to be nice. Julie called just before we ate. Now it's all over with Ade, she's interested in family life: hers and other people's. (Is that what it's like with boyfriends? They take you away, gradually, until you're too far to go back?) She said she'd had a "heart-to-heart" with Uncle Bert.

"Fact is," she said, "we had nothing to do with any

of it. Turns out it really was just French lessons. Bit of a flirt on the side, a few free dinners, but nothing serious. It only went on while Sue was away. As my mom says, he always has to have someone to cook his meals. We're not the matchmakers we thought we were."

"But we did something, didn't we?"

"What?"

"The guy from the lingerie shop. Victor Savonaire. I mean . . ."

"What happened there, Connie?"

"Well, nothing. But The Pharmacist. I invited him for dinner and . . ."

"And?"

"And . . ."

"Nothing."

"You're right," I said, suddenly realizing the truth of the matter. It had been staring me in the face all along. I just hadn't noticed. "We haven't done a thing."

I could hear Mother and Mr. Spence laughing over the gravy in the kitchen, laughing in a way I haven't heard her laugh for a long time. Sort of relaxed. Mr. Spence: her choice. Not Bert, or Victor Savonaire, or John Leakey. Not Jack. It all seemed very sad—and very funny at the same time. It seems I hadn't been in control at all. I wasn't the wise old witch I thought I was. I was just a silly little girl, cooking up stories in my own head. I thought I knew everything. It turns out I couldn't even see what was in front of me. I didn't even know my own heart.

"You all right, Con?" Julie asked.

"I'm fine," I said. "Bit tired." After that we had one of those nice, cozy chats about last night's party. I know I hated it at the time, but in retrospect these things take on a different light. I was glad I'd gone. If only to have stories to talk about with my friends afterward. I do love Julie.

I felt more cheerful when I hung up. And I was nice at supper. Mr. Spence did his Donald Duck for Marie and gave Cyril a trick to help with his nine-times table, which he's got a block on. You do something with your fingers. Say it's three times nine? Well, hold out both your hands and put the third finger down on your left hand. Then count how many fingers you have on either side. Two on one side of the finger, seven on the other. Twenty-seven. Try it. It does actually work.

And then Mother mentioned the war being almost over at last and he said something I didn't notice at the time, but I've been thinking about since. He said, "I know they're saying it's close to finished, but I reckon it's only just beginning." And he didn't look geeky at all when he said it. He looked sort of wise. Of course, five minutes later I saw him pinch Mother's bottom in a really cheesy way, but you can't have everything.

I thought I was wise. All along I thought I was wise. I'm sitting up in the bathroom now, with the cat stretched out on the floor next to me, and I realize how naive I've been. Everyone always says how grown-up I am. But I'm not, am I? I'm younger, in the sense of maturity, than almost anyone I know. At least Delilah, even at her worst, is on some sort of learning curve. But I've been standing back, thinking of myself as somehow superior, above it all. I don't have a clue about what really matters. What was I doing thinking and worrying about Mother when I had my own life to think and worry about? Sometimes you have to learn these things the hard way. It's taken losing William to make me realize that.

Chapter Twenty-nine

WEDNESDAY, MARCH 26
My bedroom, 6:10 p.m.

I cannot believe what has just happened, or what is about to happen. I am *flying*. Actually, I won't. I'll be going by boat. I hope. I hope. I hope. Please, let it not be too late.

This is what happened. I can hardly get the words out.

When I got home from school, Mother was already back. She was sitting on the sofa, next to Mr. Spence, with a serious expression on her face. For a toe-curling moment I thought they had an announcement to make, but then I noticed she was holding something in her hand.

This diary.

People talk about wanting the ground to open and swallow them up. I wanted the roof to cave in, all the bricks and the mortar and the bunk beds in Marie and Cyril's room and Mr. Spence's tiling and plumbing to cascade down on to my head and bury me forever. I would be a monument to mortification. Parents would pass our ruined house for years to come and say to their offspring, "There lies Connie Pickles, who died of embarrassment. Let that be a lesson to you, my child. *Never write it down.*"

But Mother smiled. And she wouldn't smile if she'd read this.

"Constance," she said sternly. "What have you been hiding from me?"

I played for time. "Errr," I said.

"This, this, *this.*"

And then I realized that in her other hand was a piece of folded paper. A letter. It took a moment for it to sink in. *The French-exchange letter.* The one I'd tucked away in the back of this book all those weeks ago.

"You left your book in the bathroom," she said. "And when I picked it up to put it on the stairs up to your room, this fell out. And, I'm sorry, but I saw it was to me. . . . But, Constance, why did you not show it? Did you not want to go? It is such an opportunity and I thought that . . . I am just ver', ver', ver' surprised at you."

"I—I—I—" I stuttered. What was I to say? Lie and say I didn't want to go? Or the truth: that I was worried about money and didn't want to worry *her*. I couldn't find the words for either.

And then Mr. Spence came to my rescue. He said, "Fourteen-year-old girls have a lot on their mind, Bernadette. SATs for one thing. Maybe she just forgot. Or maybe"—he threw me a quick look—"she thought it would be too expensive."

"Well, that's ridiculous," Mother said. "We can afford it. And, anyway, there is all the money she earned herself at the drugstore."

They looked at me. I was so red I thought I might explode. The drugstore money: why hadn't I thought about that? But I wanted Mother to have it, didn't I? But . . .

"Maybe she doesn't want to go," Mr. Spence added.

"No, I do," I said, before I could stop myself. I looked at Mother. "I really do. I really, really do."

And then things started happening. Mother started ranting about the urgency and pacing the room and phoning people for numbers. I don't know how she did it, but she got on to Monsieur Baker and they had this long conversation and then she hung up and, ten minutes later, he rang back. And all the time Mr. Spence and I sat on the sofa, with our hands between our knees, not talking. I was just thinking, is this really happening to me? Is it really not too late? Am I really, really going to Paris?

When she finally put down the phone on Monsieur

Baker, she clapped her hands and started filling in the form. She said Monsieur Baker had contacted the school in Champigne, the suburb of Paris where they're all going, and there was a possibility. A family with a girl my age was being contacted. We had to fax the form as quickly as we could. She had started doing it when I plucked up the courage to say what I said next.

"Mother, don't be cross, but if I really am going to Paris, please, please can I meet my grandparents?"

She went very still, and for a few seconds didn't look up from the form. When she did her face was red. She was biting her lip. She looked at me and then at Mr. Spence and then back at me. "Your grandparents . . ." she said.

"Please. I know you're not speaking to them, but I know they've written to you and . . . well, don't you think it would be good if I did?"

She gave a very deep sigh. For a moment I thought she was going to cry. She went to the bookshelves and took something from behind some books. It was a package of letters. "Maybe," she said. "Maybe it is time . . ."

So that is that. Without meaning to, without planning it, I've done what I always wanted to do—reunite my mother with her parents. She's going to write to them and tell them to call us. When I'm in Paris—when I'm in Paris!—she feels sure they will be enchanted to meet me. I can hardly wait.

Oh no, there's the phone again. Please not bad news.

Quick PS. The phone call was for me! It was Cal, the boy *not* from the Isle of Wight, who got my number from Del. I've been asked out on my first date! Can I overcome my embarrassment at being invited to go? Got to rush to the shop to fax the form. Further reflections on my return. Back in two mins.

℘

The roof, 10 p.m.

It seems ages since I broke off writing in here, but it's only four hours. I'm on the roof now, in my spot. The world keeps spinning around on me. I feel so happy and at the same time I want to cry. I haven't decided yet about Cal from Hammersmith. He's like a nice thought I've tucked away and haven't had time to examine.

I ran to the shop. The fax machine was working but in use, so I had to hang around for a bit. And then there was a spot of bother with the code—a rogue zero—but it went through in the end. I was paying when I felt someone come up behind me and stand a bit too close. When I turned around to glare, I saw it was William.

"Getting your chocolate fix?" he said. He had his hands in his front pockets, which pushed his hips forward.

258

His hair was tousled and his cheeks had high spots of pink, like he'd been cycling fast.

I told him I was sending a fax, and then I told him why.

He didn't look cross or jealous like I thought he might. He said, "Oh, that's good. I'm glad."

He was buying a paper and some chocolate, and when he'd paid, we left the shop together and started walking back. He wheeled his bike with one hand and held the package of chocolate he'd bought out toward me with the other. I hadn't spoken to him since Sunday. I knew he'd been at Delilah's yesterday suppertime because I'd seen his bike.

"You haven't been calling for me this week," I said.

"No," he said.

"I wish you would. Next term, will you?"

"Why? Do you miss me?" He put on a stupid baby voice for this. I decided to ignore it.

"Yes," I said.

We were passing the playground at the end of his road. It was empty now, even though it was still light. The sun was shining coral pink through the big trees down by the river. The mothers had taken all their children home for supper. A plastic lidded cup lay abandoned on the merry-go-round.

I went through the gates. I didn't know if he'd follow me, but he did. He leaned his bike on the railing and we sat on the swings.

I said, "You think it's all right to go on the French exchange, then?"

"Why wouldn't it be?"

"You used to think I was a bit la-di-da about France."

"I suppose that's because I was jealous," he said.

"Jealous?"

"I think I thought you'd run away and leave me."

There was something self-mocking in his voice. Past tense. It made me feel sad and lost. He could say this because these were things he'd *felt*. He didn't feel them anymore. I used to think of William as part of me. It's why I could find him so irritating. He was mine. But swinging next to him in the park this evening, I realized that's why it hurt so much. He was separate now.

"So, how's Delilah?" I said.

"Fine."

"Do you like her?"

He shrugged. "You know I do."

"Does she like you?"

"Yeah." He laughed.

We were swinging slowly, scuffing our feet on the ground. When we were little they had asphalt there, now it's those spongy pinky-gray tiles that bow slightly beneath your shoes. I was studying the floor as we were talking, looking at the darker bit, like a dent, just under me. As I swung it would come into sight and it would go. William was just in front of me. And then I saw he began kicking the ground, digging in his heels to push himself off. He was rising up, way ahead of me.

I pushed myself off too, to try and catch up, and I was gaining height, feeling the wind rush past my ears.

"Do you love her?" I shouted.

He turned and grinned at me. We were way out of sync. When he was ahead, I was behind. When I got up, he'd gone. I was so high I could feel the chain begin to slacken at the top. I put my hand out to try and catch his to slow me down, but I kept missing. He was smiling back at me as if he knew what my question really meant, but he didn't answer. I started laughing and hung my hand out until I did reach his and then I held on to it, pulling him in time with me until we slowed together. I can still feel the cold chain tugging against the back of my arm.

We came to a stop. I sort of wanted him to kiss me again more than anything in the world. But we just looked at each other and didn't say anything. I didn't make a move. Not because I was frightened—because I'm not, not anymore—and not (shamefully, I'm sorry) because I was thinking of Delilah. But because it didn't seem necessary. I think he *knew*. And a part of me thinks that's enough. He might be The One, though it's probably too early to tell, or he might just represent something safe and secure, but one thing's for sure: he *is* my friend, my oldest, bestest friend, and I love him.

Who knows what's going to happen next. Maybe when I get back from France . . . well, we'll see. There's this date with Cal still to think about, and Delilah, and the French exchange, and the Easter holidays. But I'm not scared about any of it. I'm excited. This evening we just sat there, holding hands, as the sun slipped into the river, watching the bluey-green patches between the trees go gray, and I've never felt so happy in my life.

I'm writing this on the roof, listening to the traffic in the distance as the spring sky darkens above my head and the velvet patches of night fall between the blossom and bright new leaves in the gardens below. Oh dear, poetry again. It's warm. I'm in my old men's PJs, but no bathrobe or socks.

I saw the news earlier and the war is definitely over— for now at least. Maybe Mr. Spence is right and it's only just beginning. I suppose there are no endings and beginnings in things like that. They had these pictures on the television of these ordinary people dancing in the street, and some of them were children in school uniforms, and it made me realize that the people over there are just like us. All along I've been thinking about our suburb and how far away it is, how cut off it is, from the rest of the world, from the war, when, of course, the world is made up of thousands, millions, trillions, of suburbs just like this. We're all interconnected. We all fit in.

Oh, it's so heavenly out here this evening. It's the sort of evening Granny Enid would say she'd want to bottle. I wonder, if I concentrate very hard, I can brand how I feel now on my brain so that when I'm older, when I've found out all the things there are to know, when I really am as wise as I used to think I was, I'll look back and remember how I feel tonight with my whole life ahead of me.

I don't believe it! I've just seen William. He's on his roof. He must have climbed out of the bathroom window, and now he's hanging on to the chimney, leaning out and waving. I just stood up, so I could wave too. It felt precarious; there was nothing to hold on to. I had to lean back against the window, but it was wonderful. I could see William waving at me, and I was smiling so hard I thought my face was going to break. When you stand up, I never realized, you can see across the roofs of the houses on his street to the river. You can see the bridge and the tower blocks beyond. And beyond that London, Paris, les de Bellechasses. There's William, *my* William, waving at me like the crazy boy he is, and behind him, stretching out for miles and miles, is the whole rest of the world.